Bridge to Fruition

Pawleys Island Paradise, Book 4

Laurie Larsen,
EPIC Award-winning author of *Preacher Man*

Random Moon Books
A Phase for Every Fancy

Bridge to Fruition

All Content by author Laurie Larsen
Cover Art by Steven Novak
Formatting by Polgarus Studio
Published by Random Moon Books
Published in the United States of America

Chapter One

Jasmine Malone was dashing from her dorm room when her cell phone buzzed. She groaned. She was already running late. And the last time she'd had her massage appointment, Susan warned her that if she was late again, she'd cut the appointment short. That would simply not do. Those muscle kinks following a week of finals were *not* going to relieve themselves.

Jasmine raced to her car and jumped in. Pointedly ignoring whoever was trying to contact her, she shoved into drive and was on her way, only slightly above the speed limit.

Susan was a lifesaver. Jasmine had discovered her two years ago, and had booked monthly massages ever since. Her life as a busy college student at Cornell landed her stress directly in her neck and shoulders, and an hour with Susan kept her loose and relaxed. Now, all that was separating her from graduation was the arrival of her parents.

All of them. That is, her mom and new husband Hank. And her dad, who found himself solo, since his dalliance which had broken up their marriage, was now splits-ville. She had no clue how to deal with this dysfunctional family dynamic. Hence, one last appointment with Susan.

She screeched into the salon parking lot and ran up the stairs to the salon. Was she late? She glanced at her phone and saw that no, she was right on time. The receptionist asked for her name.

"Jasmine Malone. I have an appointment with Susan."

The girl tapped on her keyboard and looked up. "Oh, didn't you get our text? Susan isn't here today. "

Jasmine frowned, hit the messaging icon on her phone and saw that indeed, the text had been from the salon. They'd sent her three today. She opened the latest message quickly. "Your appointment this afternoon will be with Dax instead of Susan."

"Wait, w———, Dax? What exactly is a Dax?" She pulled her attention from her phone to the woman behind the desk.

"Dax is one of our licensed masseuses. He's very good, actually."

Jasmine glared at her and the girl's cheeks turned a shade of pink. "What happened to Susan?"

"She had a family emergency." The receptionist cleared her throat, patted her cheeks and let her eyes rest on Jasmine. "Would you like your massage with Dax?"

Jasmine sighed. On the one hand, she had a rule about her masseuses: females only. She wasn't entirely sure why. But she thought it had something to do with the fact that under the flimsy sheet, she'd be totally naked. And the masseuse would, of course, have his hands all over her.

And she just wasn't comfortable with that.

On the other hand, she was tense and tight at the prospect of entertaining her parents on their first encounter since their divorce last summer. And it was her who'd brought them together. Well, her graduation.

So, she did a mental coin toss and decided, "Okay, yes. Dax it is."

"He'll be out in just a second."

Jasmine nodded and sat down, picked up a fashion mag and started flipping through it. A few minutes passed and she heard a deep, rumbling voice that caused a trembling in her stomach. "Jasmine?"

She looked up and her heart jumped into her throat. Tall, lean, thin-hipped. Wavy brown hair, shoulder length. Smoldering brown eyes and just a hint of whisker on his chin and lip. He was dressed in white scrubs and his tanned skin glistened in contrast.

The man was gorgeous. Her voice had disappeared. As had her mind. What had he said?

"Jasmine?" he said again, this time looking directly at her.

Jasmine darted her gaze around the waiting room. There was only one other person sitting, besides her, and it was a woman her mom's age. She cleared her throat and said a quick prayer for God to help her act normal and not embarrass herself. She had, after all, seen her fair share of handsome men before. She'd done a fashion internship in Paris last summer, for goodness sake. She'd dressed male models and helped them change clothes backstage at fashion shows. She could do this.

Of course, 90% of those men were gay. But still.

"Yes," she said, probably a trifle too loud. She cleared her throat again and said softer, "That's me." She rose and approached him.

He smiled and held his hand out. "Good afternoon. I'm Dax."

Heat flooded her cheeks, a sure sign that she was blushing. "Nice to meet you," she muttered.

"Right this way."

She followed him. They went through a labyrinth of narrow hallways until Dax opened a door and led her into a small room with a massage table in the middle, a chair in one corner and a counter and sink in another. "Have a seat, please," he said, motioning to the chair. He pulled out a folder and glanced at it. "One hour relaxation massage."

"Yes."

"You get them monthly? Very good, very good."

Her heart rate increased. "Can we just get started?"

His head darted up. "Of course. Do you have any problem areas I should be aware of?"

She took a deep breath. "Not really. I just finished finals so I'm sure my neck and shoulders are tight. All that studying, you know."

He nodded. "Oh, you're a student?"

"Not for long. I'm graduating tomorrow from Cornell."

He smiled and the sheer beauty of it almost made her swoon. "Congratulations."

"Thanks," she said and looked down at her lap.

"I'd love to go to college, but haven't had the chance yet."

She looked back up at him. "Didn't you go to massage school?"

He nodded. "Yes, that was an eleven-month program. Very intense. But I'd like to start my own massage studio someday. Hire several therapists and offer all kinds of massage. I'd need a Business degree to do that."

Okay, this was helping. Her heart rate was slowing and she felt a little more relaxed, getting to know him a little.

"I'll leave and you take everything off. Lay on the table face down and drape the sheet over you."

So much for feeling relaxed. Her pulse flew through her veins and she saw a few spots in front of her eyes. "You know, I'm not sure I can do this."

He gave her a concerned look. "What do you mean?"

She gave a nervous chuckle. "I mean, you're a man." She exhaled air. "Well, obviously you're a man. You know that, and I know that. But I've only ever had massages from women. So I'm not sure I'm comfortable with …"

"Ahhh. You're modest. That's okay. I won't see anything private, I promise. And there are benefits from getting massages from a man." He held up all ten fingers for her to see. "Strong hands. They can go forever."

Oh boy. Just the thought of Dax's strong hands and long fingers all over her body, going forever, caused her face to flood heat again. "I just remembered. I'm late for an appointment. I'm sorry."

She stood and headed for the door. But his face fell and he looked actually … heartbroken. Crestfallen. She stopped.

"No, no, it's okay. I understand." His head dipped as he made a notation in her file and closed it. "Thank you for your time." He turned and started toward the door.

Something in his dejected stance gave her a change of heart. "Dax, it's not you. Really."

He held a hand up and shook his head. "It's tough for male masseuses. Men often don't want to be massaged by a man. They prefer a woman. And women often don't want to be massaged by a man, either. Until I build up a clientele, I don't get a lot of business. But without doing a lot of business, I can't build up my clientele." He shrugged and opened the door.

"I'll do it," she said quickly before she changed her mind. "I'll do the massage."

"You will?" His beaming smile looked so happy she almost closed her eyes to block the view. A smoldering Dax was hard enough to resist. But a happy, ecstatic Dax was nearly impossible.

"Yes. I'll get undressed and scoot under the sheet. Give me five minutes. But no touching anywhere that you shouldn't, you got that?"

"Of course not! I'm a professional." He gave an excited little bow and backed out the door.

* * *

An hour later, Dax was wrapping up her massage. She had to admit, he was right about one thing: his hands were stronger than Susan's and she was the beneficiary of one awesome rubdown. She'd never felt looser or more relaxed.

He'd put her in a wonderful trance-like state with the darkened room, the peaceful music and ocean waves emitting from the sound system, his words spoken only in a whisper. Her brain was encased in a bubble that peacefully popped when he said, "All good? I'm done now. Take your time and dress when you're ready. I'll meet you out front."

She pried her relaxed eyes open only to hear the door close behind him as he crept out. She took a deep breath and sighed it out. She felt good. Relaxed, no tension, no worries. Same as when Susan would finish a massage. But ... different.

With Susan she never had to worry about the intense physical attraction that she had felt with Dax. Man, that boy was good-looking. Although she'd spent most of their hour together with her eyes closed, she pulled up a pretty accurate memory of his looks. She wouldn't mind running her fingers

6

through those waves of chestnut on his head. Soft, she imagined his hair was very soft, although perfectly rumpled and casual with no styling required. And while she was up there …

His face. She'd trail her fingers from his locks to his cheeks, run them over his prominent cheek bones, then down his jawline to …

His lips. He'd smile when her fingers reached them – maybe he was slightly ticklish there – but his stunning warm smile with his white teeth would cause her to move closer, with her own lips. Closer, closer till they were a breath away from touching. And then they'd …

Kiss. Faintly at first, feeling each other out, figuring out what they both liked, how the other tasted, this intimate connection, mouth to mouth. His lips would be soft, she decided, and his mouth would taste fresh like mints or chocolate or coffee. All her favorite things. The kiss would incite flutters in her stomach, and her heart, and she'd have to pull back to catch her breath by holding …

His shoulders. His strong, lean, muscular shoulders, leading to his arms. Oh, how she could run her hands up and down his arms to feel every inch of their form.

Suddenly, the room lightened, followed by a gasp and an "Oh, I'm so sorry, I thought you'd left already. Take your time."

It wasn't Dax's voice, at least. It was a woman's, probably the next masseuse scheduled to use this room, intending to prepare the room for her client. Not realizing that this particular customer would be lying there – how long *had* she been lying here anyway? – following her massage that, let's face it, she didn't even want in the first place, when she'd found out that Dax would be administering it.

7

Oh, how wrong she was.

Reluctantly, she dragged her legs out from under the sheet, maneuvered to a sitting position and hopped off the table. She made her way over to her clothes and began putting them on. Her fantasy of the good-looking masseuse caused her a little bit of embarrassment, knowing that she'd have to face him in mere seconds when she went out to pay her bill. And tip him. *Here's a ten, not only for the massage but the delicious fantasy afterward.* Her challenge now would be not letting on that she'd spent the last few moments dreaming about him.

She left the room and made her way down the hall, repeating a silent mantra, *Stay calm, stay cool.* She arrived at the front desk, and there he was, in all his splendor, preparing her bill. Probably the best way to proceed was to avoid looking at him as much as possible. Then maybe he wouldn't notice the evidence of her attraction: could he tell that her heart was racing, and her breath was catching at the mere sight of him?

"Thank you for coming today," she heard him say. He pushed an invoice into the line of sight of her averted head.

"Thank you, nice job," she murmured, not wanting to be rude. She pulled out her credit card and handed it to him, trying to ignore the fact that their fingers brushed against each other. Fingers touching. Shouldn't be any big deal, considering he'd spent the last 60 minutes rubbing his hands over practically every inch of her body. So why did that mere finger brush cause a physical reaction in her?

Best to get out of there as quickly as possible. Then she could get home, get on with her life, her graduation, her impending parents' meeting, her successful exit from college life. And she'd never see Dax, Susan, or this salon again.

He handed her something to sign, she signed it, and shoved her card back into her wallet. "Okay thanks again, bye." She turned and headed to the door, congratulating herself on a successful exit.

"Oh, one moment, please," she heard Dax say, but she kept moving. She was so over this little crush-moment and wanted to put it behind her. She was on the verge of major changes in her life. Time to get on with them.

She waved and headed out the door. She had reached the sidewalk when she realized he'd followed her out the door and was now standing outside on the top step of the salon. "Jasmine, wait … I wanted to give you your …"

She'd turned as he said her name, and again her heart fluttered like it had never seen a gorgeous, handsome man before, and since she was a fair distance away, and he wouldn't be able to see her reaction clearly, she allowed herself one last opportunity to admire the sight of him, speaking to her.

And then, her body was thrown violently to the pavement, a crash of pain went through her forehead and all went black.

Chapter Two

"Oh my God!" Dax shouted. "Jasmine!"

He ran down the steps and covered the short distance to the girl laying on the pavement. He laid his fingertips on her neck, found a weak pulse, then looked up. "Hey man!"

The bicycle rider who'd slammed into Jasmine, knocking her unconscious, had also landed on the pavement, thrown from his bike. He was conscious, however, and now was cautiously standing, inspecting his bloody knees and elbow.

"Get over here!"

He looked like some sort of bike delivery worker, judging from the messenger bag slung over his chest, which had spilled papers and documents all over the sidewalk. Or maybe he was a student, like Jasmine, on his way to deliver his final thesis paper to a professor. But to the guy's credit, he ignored the loose papers littered all over, and darted over to where Dax kneeled over his sleeping beauty.

Dax shook his head of that thought. She wasn't sleeping, she was knocked unconscious. And although she was surely a beauty, she wasn't his.

"I thought she was heading toward the street. She just stopped suddenly on the sidewalk and I ran right into her. I didn't mean to …"

Dax looked over at the panicked young man. "No, it was an accident, man. But I need you to call 911. Do you have a phone on you?"

The young biker stared, wide-eyed for a second, then patted his shorts pocket. "Yeah, but where?" He stood and took a few steps to where his papers were starting to scurry across the area due to wind. "Here!" He leaned and retrieved his cell phone from the grass beside the sidewalk. It must have flown out of his pocket when he fell.

While the guy called for help, Dax turned his attention back to Jasmine. She was breathing shallowly, blood dripped from a cut on her forehead but fortunately, not a heavy flow like many head wounds. Although she'd fallen hard after the impact from the bike, a cursory inspection revealed that all her limbs were unharmed. Although once she got to the ER, the doctors could decide for sure. It was her unconsciousness that worried him the most.

Dax overheard the biker giving the salon's address over the phone, then he disconnected the call and came over. "They'll be here in five."

"Thanks. You okay?"

He shrugged. "Nothing compared to her. Few scrapes, got the wind knocked out of me. I'll be fine."

Dax said, "You might as well get checked over, too."

The young man shook his head. "I don't have any insurance. I'll go if I have something wrong, but not just for a skinned knee."

Dax knew the feeling. He was uninsured as well. It was hard going these days for people of his age group — finishing school when there wasn't much money in the coffers. Finding a decent job that paid a living wage. Getting the benefits needed for insurance and retirement. He was living paycheck to paycheck — heck, he was living massage to massage. Until he could build his reputation and clientele, he'd have to just be careful and hang on.

The biker had walked over to his bike, picked it up and was inspecting it for damage. It looked okay, although one of the fenders was now scraping against the tire. He tugged at it and pulled it off. "Guess this isn't vital." He walked over to a trash container a half block down and tossed it in, came back. He kneeled and gathered his pages, stuffed them back into his bag.

"You got this?" he asked Dax.

Dax looked up, waved a hand. "Yeah. I'll wait for the ambulance and go with her."

The guy nodded and threw a leg over his bike. Hesitating, he reached into his bag and grabbed a pen and a scrap of paper. He jotted on it and handed it to Dax. "Just in case you need me for anything. But you agree it was an accident, right? Nothing I could've done?"

Dax glanced at the paper, containing the rider's name and phone number. "Yeah. In fact, it was my fault. I distracted her while she was walking away so she didn't see you coming." Trying to build his business, he had intended to hand her his card, so she'd call and request him specifically next time. He'd spent a hundred bucks on professional business cards, hoping they'd result in added clients. Not an injury for a pretty girl who'd taken a chance on him.

Satisfied, the biker rode off.

As he waited, he settled into a sitting position beside her on the sidewalk. He knew never to move an injury victim in case of serious back injury, and she wasn't awake to tell him what hurt and what didn't. But she certainly didn't look comfortable contorted on the hard cement. He caressed her face with his fingers, hoping that somehow she could feel the comfort he was trying to bestow.

The ambulance arrived, and s sudden bustle of activity brought Dax to his feet. EMTs jumping out from the front and back of the vehicle, a stretcher pulled out, the wheels popped into place underneath it. Two stocky men taking charge, kneeling beside Jasmine on the pavement, straightening her neck, lifting her onto the stretcher, strapping her in.

"Do we have an ID on the victim?" one of the men asked him.

"Yes. Jasmine …," he glanced down at her credit card receipt he'd stuffed into his pocket, since she'd left without it, "Malone. She's a customer at the salon." He gestured behind him. "They probably have full records on her, name, address and phone number anyway."

They loaded her onto the emergency vehicle and Dax hovered near the door, looking in.

"You coming with her?"

He didn't hesitate. "Yes." He noticed her purse sitting close by on the grass, grabbed it, then jumped into the back of the truck.

It wasn't till they were pulling into the hospital parking lot moments later that he realized a few things. First, he hadn't told his employer that he was leaving. Second, he was missing his next massage appointment. And third, he'd left his cell phone behind the front desk.

He quickly opened Jasmine's purse and located her phone. He pulled it out and dialed the salon's number by memory. He got Melinda, the receptionist.

"Hey, it's Dax."

"Dax, where are you? You just disappeared. Your next appointment is waiting on you, and you know we're short-handed today."

"I'm sorry. When my last client, Jasmine left, she got hit by a bike rider on the sidewalk. She's unconscious."

"Oh, my gosh!"

"I got in the ambulance and rode to the hospital with her. I'd like to stick around until she at least comes to, and I know what her injuries are."

Melinda sighed. "Okay, I guess I'll rearrange your other appointments. I'll try to get them covered, or ask them to reschedule."

"Thank you, Melinda, you're the best." He hung up, trying not to think about the loss of income and potentially long-term clientele he was risking. He was doing the right thing.

The EMTs whooshed Jasmine into the Emergency Room. Dax was following them when one of them pointed to a seat in the waiting room and ordered, "You stay here. They'll keep you posted."

He nodded and stood for a moment before taking a seat. He dropped Jasmine's purse on the chair beside him and settled in.

* * *

The clock on the wall indicated he'd been waiting almost ninety minutes when the person behind the desk said, "Excuse me, are you here for Jasmine Malone?"

He stood. "Yes."

She nodded and stepped into the waiting room. "I can take you back to see her now."

Dax followed her through a big swinging door into the curtain-separated cubicles of patients.

"Here she is, number five." The nurse pushed back the curtain to reveal Jasmine, lying on a hospital cot, her forehead wrapped impressively with gauze, and other than that, looking perfectly healthy.

"The doctor will be with you soon to talk about releasing her." The nurse walked away.

Dax made his way carefully around the bed. An IV tube connected to her arm and another one made its way into her nose, oxygen, he assumed. A little start of a bruise decorated the skin under one eye. He sank into the guest chair, reached up and took her free hand into his. "Hey, you gave me quite a scare there."

She gave him a sad smile. "Sorry 'bout that."

He shook his head. "No need for you to be sorry. Seriously. I need to apologize to you. Your accident was all my fault."

She frowned. "I don't remember much of anything."

"You had left the salon after our massage, but you didn't take your receipt. So I followed you out and called to you — just in time for you to get hit by an oncoming bike rider."

"A bike? I feel like I was hit by a truck! A bike is a much less impressive story than I had worked up in my head." Her fingers came up and found the mound of gauze taped to her forehead. "Do you believe this?"

"You were bleeding. I think your head against the pavement was your first impact."

She shook her head gently. "I have a pounding headache, but they put something in my IV for that so hopefully it'll take effect soon."

"Do you have a concussion?"

15

"Not that they can tell, but they advised me not to sleep for at least eight hours, just in case."

He squeezed her hand, grateful that she was talking normally. "Any other injuries?"

"Nope. They took x-rays of my leg because it was hurting me, but no broken bones. Thank God."

"Yeah. He was watching over you. Could've been a lot worse." Dax watched as she stared vacantly at the bed in front of her. "I'm sorry I distracted you. Can you forgive me?"

Her eyes moved to his slowly. Her lips twitched into what she probably intended as a smile but was more of a grimace. "Nothing to forgive you for. It was an accident. You didn't call my name, hoping that an oncoming bike rider would plow right into me. Right?"

A wave of relieved laughter escaped his lips. "Right. Thanks for being understanding. Tell you what, your next three massages will be free."

She smiled lazily at him. It occurred to him that she may be under the relaxing influence of pain killers. "I won't be around to claim them. After I graduate, I'm going back home."

A surprising stab of disappointment hit him. She was leaving the area. Why hadn't he thought of that when she mentioned she was graduating from college? And it wasn't just the disappointment of losing a client, either. It was more than that. It was the disappointment of losing … a potential person in his life. "Where's home?"

She stared at him, as if he'd stumped her. "Well, good question. I don't know."

Dax frowned and looked around for a nurse call button. Whoa. The girl had a head injury and now couldn't tell him where her home was?

She must've read his distress and chuckled. "No, I mean … I don't have a home, really. Or, I have two homes. Depending on how you look at it."

He leaned closer to her. "You're going to have to explain yourself, or else I'm calling the authorities."

She smiled. "My parents got divorced last summer. They sold my childhood home in Pittsburgh. My dad's living in a small but high-scale luxury condo. He has a bedroom for me there, but it's empty. I mean, it has a bed and a dresser, but not much else. It's sterile, you know? Not homey at all. My mom moved to South Carolina, bought a big old house on the beach and got remarried. There's lots of comfy bedrooms there, and I'm sure they wouldn't mind if I moved in temporarily. But … I need to do my job search. I need to work on my resume and start looking for something to do in the fashion industry. I assume I'll wind up in New York City, but it's a hard field to break into. I'd start anywhere." She closed her eyes briefly, then pried them open again. "I'm in flux."

He watched her eyes drift shut again. He looked at the meds flowing into her veins, probably causing drowsiness. However, if they'd told her not to sleep, those relaxing side effects weren't helping her any. Her face looked so peaceful, and so beautiful, despite the bandage and bruising. She possessed a natural beauty, not a lot of makeup on to cover her gleaming, healthy skin. Her features were pronounced but unenhanced. He pictured her as a happy, beautiful farm girl, exuding the glow of living a healthy, natural lifestyle.

She may be in flux, but this girl had a lot going for her and although he barely knew her, he was confident she'd land on her feet. Unlike himself, who'd had to battle complications and challenges. The jury was still out on whether he'd make his dreams actually come true.

The thought of her graduation led to his thinking about logistics concerning her family — people to contact and inform about her current whereabouts. Besides, giving her the job of talking to people would help her stay awake, per doctor's orders.

He nudged her arm, "Hey, sweetheart. Jasmine. Wake up."

She did, her eyes rolling slightly before moving in his direction and focusing on his face. Her expression became an eyebrows-up question.

"Shouldn't you call your parents and let them know what happened?"

Ahh, that brought her back to reality. "Oh, yeah. Man. They're arriving into town today, checking into the hotel. Oh, shoot." Her head darted around. "Where's my phone? My purse? I must have dropped it outside the salon."

Dax smiled, the hero of the day, at least in this brief moment. He picked up the purse he'd set on the floor beside him and held it into her view.

"You got it! Thank you!" She reached and he delivered, and she dug into the big leather bag. She located her phone, pulled it out, and although she was sitting two feet from a sign that said, "Please make your cell phone calls in the waiting room," he didn't stop her.

She pushed a few buttons and lifted it to her ear. She rested her gaze on him, an expectant smile, then a roll of her eyes. "Yeah, hi, Mom. I was hoping you'd pick up. Okay. Call me back on my cell as soon as you can. I have something to tell you that I don't want to leave in a voicemail."

She tried again, and this time he guessed that she connected with her father. "Hey Dad, where are you?" She waited a beat. "Oh, that's close. You're about twenty minutes out. Uh huh. Yeah. Listen Dad, I have some news. I just got into a minor accident. No, no, not a car accident. I was a pedestrian, crossing the sidewalk when I got hit by a bike rider. Yeah. Crazy, huh? No, I'm fine. I'm in the ER, in fact. Yeah, that's what I was thinking, you could just come here." She listened for a moment, then a frown marred her perfect face. She pulled the phone away and addressed him. "What's the name of this hospital?"

He told her, and she repeated it to her father.

"I was knocked out when my head hit the pavement. But that's about it. Concussion watch for a few hours, no broken bones. Yeah. But I'll have a nice shiner for my graduation ceremony. Yes, lovely. No, don't worry. I'll be fine, especially with my daddy around to watch after me." She looked up Dax and winked at him. "Okay, see you then."

She disconnected the call and explained, "My dad's a doctor. He'll get whatever information we need out of this crew." She chuckled and then her cell sounded. It was her mom. She repeated the story, but this time, there was a lot more reassurance that she was fine, she was safe, no residual injuries and all would be all right. When she hung up with her mom, she took a big breath and sighed it out.

He leaned in closer and without thinking, he took her two hands in both of his and squeezed them. Her skin was soft as velvet, but of course, he knew that, having spent an hour with his hands all over her. Her eyes looked alarmed before they settled into acceptance of his gesture.

"This is it. The first time my mom and my dad will be in the same room together since their divorce."

His thumbs massaged her hands and she closed her eyes, melting into the pleasure. "Are you afraid they'll make a scene?"

Her eyes flew open. "No, no, they're both much too civilized for that. But I know they're both going to feel awkward, not quite sure of what the other one is thinking. I mean, after they sold the house, they've had no reason to be in touch with each other. It's been a totally clean break."

Dax listened to her talk a little bit about her parents' divorce. He could relate to a broken family, but not due to a divorce. He was a child of the system — given up for adoption, moved from one foster home to another, always in search of love and acceptance. It wasn't the standard way to grow up, and certainly not the best, but he'd gotten through, relatively unscathed, and graduated now to being an adult with his own future to build.

She quieted and pulled her hands away from his massaging thumbs. He took a hint and stood. "I'll let you get ready for your parents."

She looked for a moment like she would protest, but then she squeezed her mouth shut and nodded her head. "I can't thank you enough for helping me. I don't know where I would be without you calling the ambulance and making sure I got here safely."

He shook his head. "Least I could do." He edged backward to the curtain entrance, his heart feeling unusually heavy at the thought of leaving her. Disappointment that this would be the last time he ever laid eyes on her beautiful face. And a sense of loss that his life wouldn't include a place in it for her. If only they'd met under different circumstances.

If he didn't force himself to create a distance between the two of them, he knew he would want to reach out to her, to kiss her, to caress her angel face. So he made his feet head for the door, where he could give a casual wave and say a fond farewell. Like he met beautiful, happy, smart girls every day who made his heart twist at the thought of saying good-bye.

"Daddy!" she said suddenly, and he turned to see a tall, well-dressed, put-together man duck easily into the curtained cubicle.

Chapter Three

"I'd hate to see the other guy."

Her dad had used that same line at least a half dozen times that she could remember during her childhood. Once when a softball had made an errant bounce in the dirt by first base and she didn't have her glove in place. Once when she was the top of the cheerleader pyramid and instead of catching her, Tommy Latke had let her fall on the gym floor, face first. And other miscellaneous mishaps during her childhood as a tomboy. He probably thought it was funny and original, and she didn't have the heart to tell him it was his most oft repeated corny line.

"Hardy har har." She reached her arms out to hug him, but he was more interested in her bruises and her bandages. First things first. She supposed she couldn't blame him.

He pressed on the bruise under her eye, firm but gentle. His fingers walked lightly across the length of it. Then he turned his attention to the bandage. He tugged at it, and removed the whole thing. She studied him as he examined her, hoping to see some reaction to her injured face; some way to judge if she was in medical trouble or not. Her dad spent his days taking care of others, and he'd taken care of her his whole life. But his expression was the medical equivalent to a poker face — nothing revealed there. He turned his attention to the knot on her forehead, kneading it gently with his fingertips, then brushed over the three short stitches required by her wound. Finally satisfied, he curled his mouth into a closed smile and his eyebrows went up as he nodded at her.

"Looks fine, sweetie."

He went into the corner of the cubicle and came back with fresh gauze and tape, and before she knew it, he'd finished wrapping her up.

"Can you spare a hello hug and kiss now? Geesh."

He smiled and leaned his torso over her bed and pulled her into a warm hug. She closed her eyes and then a short clearing of the throat sounded from the corner.

Dax. He was still here. He'd been about to leave when Dad showed up.

"Oh!" She pulled out of the hug and smiled at Dax. "Daddy, I want to introduce you to my savior. The man who called the ambulance and made sure I got here safely. Dax … um, I'm sorry, I don't know your last name, do I?"

"Murphy. Dax Murphy. Nice to meet you." He held a hand out to her dad, who accepted the handshake.

"Thank you, thank you very much." Dad reached into his pocket and pulled out his wallet. His go-to reward for anyone doing him a service. Hand over a couple twenties and another verbal expression of gratitude. "We appreciate your help, we really do."

Dax gave the bills in Dad's hand a quizzical gaze. "No, no, I don't need …"

"Just a token of our appreciation. Please, take it."

Dax gave his head a firm shake and met eyes with her dad. "No. Thank you, though."

Her dad directed his confused gaze at her.

23

"That's okay, Daddy. He's a ... friend." Was he? She'd known him all of about four hours, one of which she was paying him to massage her. And yet, he'd felt compelled to not only call the ambulance, but to jump into the back of it with her, missing the remainder of his shift, and most likely, blowing off several appointments, to come to the hospital with her and make sure she was all right. Was that the act of a friend? Or just a concerned service provider?

Or, was it something more?

Her dad was still looking at her. "He called the ambulance for me and waited for me while I was getting treated."

"Yes." He turned back to Dax and tried again, holding the bills out in his direction. "I'd just feel better about compensating you for your time. Pay for your cab back to work. Reimburse you for any missed work time."

"It's not necessary."

Jasmine was just feeling sorry for him — her dad could be awfully persuasive, and obviously he didn't feel comfortable taking the compensation — when just then, her mom ducked into the cubicle under the hanging curtain. She directed her gaze on Jasmine in the bed and covered the short distance in a few steps, pulling her into arms Jasmine knew from a thousand lifetime hugs. No, a million, at least. Her mom was one of the most loving and affectionate people she'd ever known, and Jasmine'd never stopped giving thanks that she was lucky enough to have her for a mom.

"Mom!" she managed into her mom's shoulder. The embrace went long and when her mom finally pulled away, Jasmine saw tears in her eyes. "Ahh, Mom, don't worry. I'm fine."

Leslie pulled in a ragged breath and let it out. "Look at you! Hit by a bike! Knocked unconscious! Oh, child!"

"I'm just glad it wasn't a car," Jasmine joked.

Her dad cleared his throat. "I did a quick examination, Leslie, and I'm convinced that they've treated her appropriately."

Jasmine could feel her mom's tensing, as well as see it. Her shoulders went tight, her face froze in the expression it was sporting when her dad had spoken up. Which was sort of a Joker from Batman-style grimace.

Then, her mom recovered nicely, intentionally. She looked over at him as if she'd just noticed that he stood there and said with a practiced air of calm, "Oh, hello, Tim."

The exchange marked the first time since her parents' divorce last summer that either of them had spoken to the other. Sort of a moment for the family annals, Jasmine guessed.

Her dad tensed then. Poor guy, Jasmine could tell he was out of his element and wasn't quite sure what to do, a dilemma that hardly ever smudged her confident, in-charge father. Did he go over to her and give her a hug? A handshake? Did he stay where he was and not deign to touch this woman he'd been married to almost twenty years, the woman he shared a daughter with? The relationship he'd broken apart a year ago, because he'd ventured into another one that he thought was better suited to him, at that time of his life?

The answer became clear when Hank Harrison, Leslie's new husband, emerged through the curtains and entered the cubicle. His entrance was like a deep breath during a yoga class — a cleansing, relaxing, healthy pull of air into a body starving for it. Hank was one of the best men in the world. Jasmine had known this since the first day she'd met him, and obviously her mom knew it, too. They were newlyweds, married a short time after Leslie's divorce from Tim. But sometimes love was just meant to be. Sure, they could've waited a "reasonable" amount of time after the divorce, and after their first date. But why? Hank and Leslie made each other happy. They were two souls who needed the other. And it didn't take much convincing for them to commit to each other.

"Hi, doll," Hank said as he focused on Jasmine, a slight smile on his face mixed with pity evident in his creased forehead.

"Hi, Hank."

"Sorry about your accident. The doc says you're doing fine though, huh?"

That's why he hadn't come in right away. He was tracking down a doctor. He was such a good dad. He couldn't help but exude love and support for the children in his life — three of his own, and now, Jasmine too.

"Yeah, I guess I just wanted to stand out at graduation tomorrow."

"Well, darlin', you didn't have to go to this trouble. You were already gonna be the most beautiful girl in the place. Well, beside your mother."

His southern drawl washed over her, making her miss the low country of South Carolina and the sandy white beaches and waves where he and her mom lived together in a beachfront old house on stilts.

Her dad stepped forward then, and the difference between the two men — the two fathers in her life — became ultimately clear. Her dad — the successful, educated, intelligent doctor, dressed in an impeccably tailored suit. Handsome, clean-shaven and groomed. Very capable, very accomplished.

And Hank — dressed in khaki cargo shorts and a golf shirt, untucked, and an old baseball cap over his grown out hair. A lookalike of the actor who played Indiana Jones, he was casually handsome, but didn't put a bit of effort into making himself that way. Never afraid to show his affection for those he loved. His heart out on his sleeve, willing to go any lengths.

Just as Jasmine was wondering about introducing the two men, her mom stepped up. "Tim, this is my husband." She paused a long moment, letting that reality float out into the room. "Hank Harrison."

Her dad took that punch to the gut in stride, his widening eyes and tightly drawn lips the only evidence of the pain the introduction had caused him. Then he held up a hand and offered it to Hank. "Nice to meet you, Hank."

Leslie continued with the joint introduction. "Hank, this is Tim … Jasmine's father."

Again, Jasmine recognized the slice caused by her mother's words. Her dad's shoulders jolted momentarily, almost invisibly, but she knew him better than anyone and understood that her mother's words, whether they were intentional or not, hurt him. Like all he was left to Leslie was the father of her one treasured child. After twenty years together, wasn't there anything else?

But despite Jasmine's discomfort for her dad in this awkward moment, she didn't pity him, due to the role he'd played in tearing his own marriage apart. Actions have consequences. Oh yeah, Rule #1, Dad. You have an affair with a woman half your age, and you don't get to keep your devoted wife of 20 years. Welcome to the real world.

Hank took a comfortable step forward and gripped Tim's hand. No discomfort there.

"Pleased to meet you, Tim." And Jasmine held back a smile at what else he could've said, but was way too much of a southern gentleman to attempt.

"Yes," her dad said in a clipped voice, his forehead creased due to the frown on his face. "Did you have a good drive up here?"

Ithaca, New York was a long way from Pawleys Island, SC, but knowing her mom and Hank, they probably filled the trip with conversation, music and laughter and enjoyed every moment together. Whereas Dad's solo trip from Pittsburgh, although shorter, was spent listening to the New York Times and some medical journal on audio book. Bore, snore.

Jasmine suddenly felt an overwhelming need to take control so her parents' first meeting was smooth, no chance for awkwardness. And no wonder — she'd been obsessed with it for the last two weeks, barely able to concentrate on her finals because her mind kept slipping back to this very moment. She didn't want to allow the two of them the time or the privacy to get into a heated discussion. Would they? Or did they want calm and civil as much as she did?

She couldn't think of any other way to take control of the room, than to re-live the moment of her accident. That topic was of interest to both her mother and her father. She could launch into a detailed story of everything she remembered, pre-collision and post-arrival at the ER, and that could easily burn ten, fifteen minutes of averted uncomfortableness.

"Hello."

Or, oh yeah, Dax was still in the corner over there by one of the machines. What kind of terrible hostess was she anyway? "Oh, my gosh, Dax. I'm so sorry. I haven't introduced you yet. Mom, Hank, this is Dax Murphy. He was the one who called the ambulance for me and got me safely here, then waited till I woke up and spoke to the doctors. He's a gem."

Dax smiled at the description, looking pleasantly surprised at her choice of words and he maneuvered around the cramped surroundings to offer a hand to both her mom and Hank, who welcomed him warmly. Amidst the "thank you's" and "thank God you were here's" being delivered by Leslie and Hank, her dad sort of faded into the background, observing. Dax smiled and darn if he didn't look so handsome, so happy and so like he fit in… to this side of the family. Leslie was giving him a hug to emphasize her thanks and he was patting her back like he didn't mind at all.

"Seems like we need to thank you properly for all your help. We need to take you out to dinner, Dax."

Dax shook his head, looked down at his feet and chuckled a little. "It was my pleasure, …"

But then Hank interrupted with, "No, now. We want to thank you and get to know you a little better. We need to eat dinner anyway, and you do too. So why not eat together? Besides, it'll be good to get acquainted before the graduation ceremony tomorrow evening."

Dax's eyes darted to hers. Hank thought Dax was a special person in her life. He must, or why would he assume Dax was invited to graduation? Or even interested in attending? If Hank thought Dax and Jasmine were together — a couple — there's a good chance that Mom thought it too.

She winked at Dax, about to let him off the hook. She opened her mouth, ready to explain to all the parents in the room, when he said, "In that case, yes, thank you. I'd love to go out to dinner with you tonight. And go to graduation with you tomorrow night."

Jasmine wasn't sure whether to call a halt to the charade or break out laughing. She actually felt more like the latter.

The ER nurse chose that precise moment to breeze in, a clipboard in hand. "I have your release papers. Here's the instructions from the doctor …" and she started reading them from the papers that would be sent home with her. Jasmine's mind was too distracted to actually follow what the woman was saying. She was thinking about Dax and the gag he was playing on her family.

Why would he do this? Did he like her? Like, in that way? Why else would he give up practically an entire afternoon of work, and now an evening to go out to dinner with her family, in addition to her graduation ceremony tomorrow evening? He couldn't be serious. If she weren't the one in the cap and gown, she'd definitely skip tomorrow's ceremony. Those things were boring …

Fortunately, her mom was looking over her shoulder at the instructions, so Jasmine let her mind continue to explore this strange turn of events. If he did like her, and that's a huge if, how would she feel about it? Happy? Giddy? Resistant? Sure, he was breathtakingly handsome with his long, wavy hair, his intense brown stare and his tall, slim body that resembled those of the models who walked the runway in Paris during her internship last summer. She'd be absolutely insane not to notice, and be interested in dating him.

But where could it lead? A big fat nowhere, that's where. She had two more days in New York, and then she was moving back to … where? Pittsburgh? Pawleys Island? She hadn't thought that far ahead. But wherever she ended up, she couldn't imagine Dax coming with her.

The instructions done, Jasmine signed her name and the nurse handed her a bag containing her clothes. Everyone except her mom shuffled out of the cubicle so she could dress. Mom helped pull her stuff out and laid it all on the cot.

"So ...," Mom said meaningfully. "Dax?" She looked directly at Jasmine and raised her eyebrows.

Jasmine giggled. "Yeah, Dax. Cute, huh?" She concentrated on pulling one piece of clothing after another onto her body. Unfortunately, all that was there was a pair of shorts, a tee shirt and a pair of flip flops so she couldn't evade Mom for long.

"Very cute. I'm just wondering why I've never heard of him before."

She had a point. She and Mom were tight. They talked, not daily, but definitely weekly, more than once. She kept Mom up to speed on her life, and Mom did the same for her. Which was why she knew that Mom was looking forward to summer break from her class of sixth graders, even though she'd had a fantastic school year. And she knew that Mom and Hank were madly in love, living in The Old Gray Barn. She knew all about Hank's daughter Marianne's new dinner theater in the Seaside Inn that she and her husband Tom owned, and how gangbusters it was going. And she knew all about her stepbrother Jeremy and his new wife Emma Jean, and their custom furniture business they just opened.

And Mom knew all about each of her classes this year, the fact that she'd struggled this semester keeping her grade point average above a 3.0, so she'd sworn off nearly all social activities, including dating. Mom knew she hadn't even started a job search, so focused was she on school, a point that Mom had even encouraged. First things first. Start the job search after graduation — no big deal.

Which was why Mom was so surprised about the unexpected presence of Dax.

"Relax, Mom. I just met him today. I went to get my last massage and Susan wasn't there, so Dax stepped in for her. Little did I know he was Mr. Tall, Dark and Gorgeous. I almost didn't let him do it. But eventually I did. It was the best massage I ever had."

Leslie smiled.

"I was leaving the salon when the bike delivery rider slammed into me, and Dax took care of everything. He hasn't left my side since."

She was ready to jump off the high cot, but Mom grabbed her arm and helped guide her off, slowly. Turns out, it was a good thing she did because her head started to pound, just from that motion.

"Sweetie, be careful. You heard the nurse. No sudden movement, especially changing heights." Mom helped her gather her purse and papers. "Sounds to me like he's interested in you."

Jasmine shrugged. "I haven't figured it out. But he lives here, and I'm moving in two days, so what's the point?"

Leslie considered that. "Can't hurt to let him come to graduation. Maybe he'll be a buffer between me and your dad."

Jasmine turned to her mom. "Yeah. Must be so awkward for you. You haven't seen him at all in almost a year. You doing okay with it?"

Mom raised and lowered one shoulder. "No way around it. Of course we both want to be here. We'll have to get used to it over the years. Family events that impact us both." They were about ready to exit the cubicle and Leslie lowered her voice and said in a stage whisper, "I'll tell you, it's a lot easier to face him with my dream husband around."

Just then, the curtain flew back and Dad pushed his way through. "Leslie, could I have a moment? Please?"

Chapter Four

Mom didn't take her hand off Jasmine's arm. If anything, she tightened her grasp. Leading her daughter to safety was Mom's top priority and nothing, not even a curt summons from her ex-husband was going to change that. Which made Jasmine a little torn.

Sure, Leslie would rather avoid confrontation with Tim. To her, Tim was now a person who was an important part of her past, but held absolutely no role in her present or her future. Been there, done that, got the tee shirt.

But she supposed her dad needed some kind of closure. Even if he didn't admit to that kind of pop psychology. He was a strong, smart, in charge guy. He was a surgeon! How much smarter can you get than that? But he'd made the biggest mistake of his life when he'd forsaken his devotion to his marriage, and he strayed and was unfaithful. People didn't find love like theirs every day. And although he was the one who'd taken up with another woman, it wasn't of the lasting variety. His temporary dalliance had dumped him, and now he'd ripped apart the marriage that he'd savored for twenty years. And now, that woman was gone too.

He was alone.

And not dealing with it well. Jasmine knew that, more from what he didn't say when she talked to him — occasionally — than what he did say. He had no idea how to talk about his mistakes and the consequences they caused in his life. Despite being super-intelligent, he was a guy, after all. A guy who never had talked about his feelings, even when his personal life was going well.

So the fact that he wanted to reach out to his ex-wife and start some sort of conversation, was a good thing. For him. Maybe not for her.

They were both her parents, and Jasmine loved them both. Who should she support in this dilemma?

"Mom," she said, patting her hand, "I'm fine to ride my wheelchair-steed out to the waiting room by myself. I'll hook up with Hank and Dax. When you're done talking to Dad, I need a ride back to the salon to get my car."

"No." Her mother said the word firmly, before she'd even finished her sentence. Okay. That was decided, then.

"Tim, whatever it is you want to talk to me about, you can say in front of Jasmine. And I'd appreciate it if you'd make it short because I need to get her back to her apartment and start following these doctor's orders." She held up the papers and shook them at him.

His eyes traveled from Leslie's to Jasmine's and back again. He cleared his throat. Hesitated. And then, "It's good to see you again. It's been a long time."

Leslie nodded.

"You look good."

"Beach living agrees with me. Always has."

"And you seem happy …?" It was a question because, Jasmine supposed, he hadn't been close enough to her in the last year to form an opinion for himself about her happiness.

"Very. And you?" Her mom was keeping it short and succinct. Very cool and calm. Jasmine was mentally taking notes, learning a technique from her mom she'd never seen her use before.

Jasmine turned her gaze over to her father when he didn't answer immediately. It would've been so easy for him to respond with a flippant, "Yeah, fine." But he didn't. Because he wasn't. And as he worked through his response, she saw his thought pattern race across the expressions on his face. Her dad had never been particularly expressive. He was digging deep and trying to open up. Trying to be honest. Because deceit is what had gotten him to this place, this time. And that obviously hadn't worked.

He finally looked up at Leslie and focused directly on her. Jasmine had the weird impression that although she was in the room, she was no longer in the room. The energy circling around them was absorbed by just her mom and her dad.

"Let's just say I'm living the life I deserve." He looked down, gathered his resolve and looked back at her, entrancing her eyes with his own. "I was awful to you, Leslie, and I never took the chance to apologize properly."

Her mom broke their stare and she put her free hand up, using it to wave the sentence away, dismissing the notion, even while her other hand gripped Jasmine's arm even tighter. "No, no. No need."

"Leslie, please. I know you don't need it. You're happy and settled into your new life. Your new … husband." He literally had to choke out that last word. "But I need to say it. Please. Just listen."

Leslie turned her head, looked at the floor, but gave a slight nod that was only detectable if someone was watching her closely. Which she and her dad were. *Go ahead.*

Jasmine looked over at her dad, mentally urging him to go, just get it over with. *Speak, man! You may not ever get this chance again.*

And still, her dad, always the slow and steady one, just stood there, forming his thoughts in his head. You woulda thought he'd already come up with the speech. Rehearsed it to pull it out when it was time.

"Leslie, what you and I had was special. I loved you from the very beginning. We went through a lot together. You sacrificed so much. You put me through med school ..."

Leslie exhaled. "Tim ..."

He nodded, catching her meaning. "I'm sorry. I'll get to the point. Which is this: I screwed up. Big time. I hate to think I was victim to such a cliché as a mid-life crisis. But that's it, entirely. I was reaching my mid-forties, my mid-life, and I looked around me and saw things that weren't there. I was bored, stuck in a rut. I wanted change, excitement."

Leslie opened her mouth and turned her head to him, about to speak, then changed her mind and stayed silent. Jasmine understood. She didn't want to get into a dialogue with him. This was his closure. She'd agreed to let him speak — to get it off his chest. Mom was going to let him do just that.

"I made the grave error of deciding I couldn't find that change and excitement with you by my side. I was under the ludicrous opinion that I needed to find another woman to help me accomplish that. And when I did, I broke my marriage vows, and I tore my family apart. For that, I will forever be sorry. Because once it's torn apart, it doesn't appear that there's any way to put that back together."

He paused and her mom came to the conclusion that he was done. "Is that all?" she said, an unmistakable chill in her voice.

"No, it isn't. I want you to know that I wronged you, and I realize it. You didn't deserve any of this. You didn't do anything wrong, Leslie, it was all me and my crazy ideas that what I had with you wasn't enough, somehow. But now that it's all gone, I'd give anything — *anything* I own — to get back what I had before. Your love, your respect, our partnership." He looked frantically around the small room, raising his hands to try to drive his point home. Jasmine's heart went out to him. "I'm alone, Leslie. I don't say that so you'll feel sorry for me. I deserve the lonely state of my life right now. I know that. I look at you with ... him ... and all the changes you made in your life to be able to make your lives together work. You gave up your life in Pittsburgh, your stable teaching job, your lifestyle. You moved to another state. And it gives me hope that someday I'll heal and recover and find love again."

Mom wasn't looking at him. She was looking at the floor but she was listening. Jasmine could tell that from the single tear that trailed down her cheek and dropped to the floor. Leslie raised her free hand and wiped the moisture from her face, cleared her throat and lifted her head to look at him. "You broke my heart, Tim. You ripped it apart. I thought I had true love with you. But you threw it away as if it meant nothing. Our lives together. It meant nothing to you."

He took two steps closer to her, reached out for her hands, but she pulled them away. "I'm sorry. I was careless with our love, with your heart, and I'm very sorry. It took me this long to know the huge mistake I made. I'll pay for that mistake for the rest of my life. But please, don't ever think that I didn't love you, or that our lives together meant nothing. You were my life, my universe, for a long time. Don't doubt that."

Leslie took a long inhale of air into her lungs, held it there and sighed it out. She met eyes with Tim and shrugged. "Okay, what now? You've finally come to your senses. You've apologized. I've moved on, but you still broke my heart."

"Can you forgive me?" Unable to touch her, he leaned in closer with his upper body so their faces were only inches apart. Jasmine realized he was putting himself out there, serving up his heart on a platter to her.

"No." Leslie looked away.

"No?" Her dad deflated. "But why? You've moved on, you said it yourself. You're happy. You've *won*, Leslie. I'm miserable, I admit it. So why can't I have your forgiveness?"

"It's not a competition, Tim. I haven't *won* because I'm happy, and you haven't *lost* because you're not happy. Do you think I want that for you? No. We've all lost. All three of us, because of what you did to us. Hank is a wonderful man." Jasmine couldn't help noticing her dad's flinch at those words but her mom soldiered on. "I'm madly in love with him, and he with me. We're meant to be together. I love our simple life at the beach. *But*. I wouldn't be there if you hadn't done what you did. I was perfectly happy with *our* life too, Tim. You destroyed that."

Her dad's head lowered, his gaze fixed on the white tile floor at his feet.

"So although I've landed on my feet, no, I don't forgive you for what you did. I can't, without God's help. I'm going to have to pray about this, asking God to get my heart to a place where I can forgive you. Because I know I should.

Jesus said it in the Bible to forgive your enemies. But frankly, I haven't spent prayers on that particular request, because I've had a lot of other things to pray about in the last year."

His words were spoken so softly, Jasmine barely heard them. "Am I your enemy, Leslie?"

But her mom heard them because she responded quickly. "No, Tim. Not anymore."

And then, Leslie turned to her, plastered a big, intentional, albeit fake smile on her face and said, "Now, we need to get this injured beauty home, and take care of her." They took a few tentative steps toward the curtain. "Tim, we'll see you at dinner at six thirty at the restaurant. Reservation is under Malone."

* * *

Dax's feet were starting to hurt — an occupational hazard for a licensed massage therapist who stood for hours at a time, working on loosening the muscles and joints of his clients. But add on top of that, the time he stood in the corner of Jasmine's ER cubicle while her various parents paraded in, and now, the extended moments he'd stood in the waiting room with her stepdad, waiting for her and her mom, when they both thought they were following right behind them.

The fact that her dad had also held back, and was missing from the waiting room as well, seemed to point to the conclusion that he had delayed the women and was probably engaging them in an uncomfortable conversation at this very moment.

Dax looked over to Hank, and saw that he had most likely come to the same conclusion himself, and was in all likelihood, running the options through his mind. A) Let his new wife talk to her ex-husband by herself, give her the privacy she might need to try to resolve whatever outstanding issues the ex wanted to discuss. Or B) wander back to the cubicle under the guise of finding out what was holding them up, and provide the support needed by his wife to deal with a potentially awkward and uncomfortable conversation with her ex.

So far, Hank had gone with Plan A. But from the looks of his furtive glances in the direction they had walked from, he was moments away from ditching it and executing Plan B.

In fact, it appeared his mind was made up when he turned and took three intentional steps in that direction — just as Leslie and Jasmine entered the waiting room, lagged by Tim.

Jasmine's mom was all business and took over as the coordinator of the next steps. "Okay, we're ready! Dax and Jasmine will ride in Hank's and my car. We'll take Jasmine back to the salon to pick up her car. Dax, do you have a car there as well?"

"Yeah."

"Good. We'll drop you off there. We'll take Jasmine back to her apartment to rest. Are you feeling up to dinner, sweetie?"

Jasmine nodded. "I think so."

"Okay. Reservations are at 6:30 at a place called Maxie's Supper Club. Dax, I'll call and increase the reservation to five if you'd like to join us."

Despite the family dynamic and the thought that maybe the four of them needed to be together without an outsider present, he still wanted to go. Really wanted to go. His brain knew that Jasmine only had a few days left in Ithaca before she moved away, but in his heart he wanted to spend as much time with her as he could.

"Yes, please."

"Okay. It's all set." Business done, Leslie and Hank headed for the door to the parking lot. Dax turned to Jasmine and held out a hand. She looked at it and smiled, then gripped it in her own, wrapping her fingers tightly between his.

They reached the car and Dax opened the back door, waited for Jasmine to climb in, then scooted in after her. He reached for her hand again since it was so comfortable holding it. But then he pulled his hand back, hoping she hadn't seen. He had a good reason for offering her a steady arm to hold onto while they walked across the parking lot. Not so much while she was seated in the car, strapped in by her seat belt. He barely knew this girl. But there was something about her that attracted him.

Well, duh. Of course she attracted him, with her long brown hair, her healthy and happy face, her petite body, with just the right amount of curves in the right places. She was adorable. She was beautiful. He'd have to be blind not to notice.

And yes, he'd had his chance to explore that body first hand when he'd massaged it earlier in the day. But he was professional and he'd purposely turned off the part of his mind — his libido — that recognized the intimacy with which he had been touching her. She wasn't his to touch in *that* way. She had been his client — paying him for a service which he'd trained and studied and practiced for. Which just so happened to involve running his hands all over her bare body, over that soft skin, those perfect curves.

Again, he turned off the switch in his brain that would continue going down that line of thought. Because the last thing he needed, or wanted, while he sat in the back seat with the girl, was a perfectly natural, but unwanted, physical reaction to those thoughts.

He cleared his throat and looked down at his leg. It was so close to hers that if he moved it just a half inch to the left, their limbs would collide. He wondered how she would react. His curiosity took over and he did — moved his leg so gently and slowly that it brushed against hers. And although his was covered with the soft cotton of his uniform, hers was bare since she was wearing shorts. At his touch, she looked down at the spot of contact and then looked at him with a smile.

And reached for his hand and pulled it into both of her own, resting them on their joined legs. He was amazed by the surge of blood his heart pumped at that moment, making him feel lightheaded. And happy.

Why? he pondered. Why did the simple act of this particular girl holding his hand make him go almost giddy with happiness? He'd had no shortage of women in his life. In fact, his phone contacts list contained at least a dozen women's phone numbers he could call up if he needed a date to an event, or just someone to spend a lonely evening with.

He forced the elation out of his face, settling it into a casually happy expression and looked over at Jasmine's face. "How are you feeling?"

"Tired. Headache. But other than that, okay."

"I'm sorry about what happened outside the salon."

She shrugged. "Wasn't your fault."

In a way, it was, and he'd never get over feeling that way. If he'd just let her pay her bill and leave the salon, like he did with every other client he'd ever worked on, he wouldn't have followed her out the door, he wouldn't have distracted her by calling her name, and she wouldn't have gotten slammed by a passing biker.

"Is that why you've stuck by my side all afternoon? Because you think this injury was your fault?"

He froze. Tough question to answer. A variation of the one he'd been asking himself all afternoon. Why had he spent his whole afternoon at the hospital, skipping out on scheduled appointments, risking getting fired for missing his shift? Was it just because of a sense of duty? Because of guilt? Or was there more to it?

Of course there was more to it. But how could he possibly tell her about his growing attraction to her without sounding like an idiot? Or scaring her away with the intensity of his feelings.

"No," he said simply. "That's part of it, but not the only reason."

"You do know that I'm leaving town for good the day after tomorrow, right?"

"Yeah, you told me."

Her thumb rubbed back and forth over the skin between his own thumb and index finger. His gaze darted to her face, but she was looking down at their hands. He made a joke out of it. "You've got some skills. I could teach you how to do massage with a technique like that."

She laughed, and stopped the rubbing. Darn.

They arrived at the salon way too soon for his liking, and they climbed out of the backseat. He thanked her mom and stepdad and stepped away. Jasmine followed him.

"Thanks for everything, Dax. The massage, for calling the ambulance, and for staying with me at the hospital. It means a lot."

"Don't mention it." Please. "I'm looking forward to seeing you at dinner tonight."

She grimaced. "Yeah, with the crazy Malone/Harrison combined parental group."

He smiled. Little did she know. She may think her family was dysfunctional or a pain, or whatever. Most everyone he knew in his age group who had family members, felt that way. But it sure as heck beat not having one at all, like him. There wasn't a single person in this world he could truly call family, other than a few people he'd stayed in touch with from his childhood in the foster care system who had made a difference, and still cared enough to pick up the phone when he called. People complaining about their families had never made sense to him — not that Jasmine had done that. But, whoever said families were perfect? Whoever led people to believe that a group of individuals, connected by blood, would get along swimmingly without an occasional reality TV-drama moment? But it was worth it in the end to have relationships with family members.

At least, he imagined it would be.

"I like your parents. All of them." He smiled. And I like you. He almost said it, but didn't get it out before she replied.

"Even my dad? Who tried to pay you off for helping me today? I hope you weren't insulted by that."

He shook his head. "Not at all. It's obvious he loves you. He wanted to reward anyone who helped you. He wasn't exactly sure who I was or what my relationship to you is." What *was* his relationship to her, he wondered, then forged on. "That's probably just his way, I'm guessing. Letting his money speak for him."

She stared at him. "You're very perceptive. I'd never thought of it that way before but that's exactly his way."

LAURIE LARSEN

"Compared to Hank and your mom, who use love and affection instead of money to get results."

She grinned. "Yep. Wow. You're going to fit right in."

His heart skipped a beat. Fit right in ... to what?

"Dinner tonight," she added as if she could read his mind. Or maybe she just read his expression brought on by her words.

"Okay," he said, wrapping it up before he said or did anything else to embarrass himself in front of this girl, "I'll meet you at the restaurant. If you want me to give you a ride home afterward, I'd be happy to."

"Thanks."

He waved at Leslie and Hank, turned and went into the salon. Melinda was behind the receptionist desk, her hair hanging in clumps around her face, like she'd been pulling at her locks.

"Dax, oh my gosh, it's about time. I had to take care of three of your appointments. Two I was able to fill with another therapist, but they were late, and had to back up their own appointments. One I couldn't fill so I had to cancel, and she wasn't very happy, believe me. I rescheduled her for next week. If she shows. If she doesn't drop us and go somewhere else." She blew a lock of hair out of her face and looked up at him. "I know you had a medical emergency with a client, Dax, but you put us in a real bind."

He sighed and came around behind the desk, scanning at her notes of the appointments he'd screwed up today. He'd call them personally, apologize for the inconvenience and offer a discount for their next massage. A discount that he would cover to the salon out of his own pocket.

No wonder he hadn't gotten into the black yet in this new business endeavor.

46

"I'm sorry. When Jasmine got hit by the biker outside the salon I felt it was my duty to ride with her to the hospital. Once I was there, I wanted to wait around and find out how she was."

Melinda looked at him. "How is she?"

"Fine. Thank God." *In fact, I'm going out to dinner with her tonight.* Well, sort of. Her and all three of her parents.

"Well Dax, Robin wants to talk to you. She's in her office."

He couldn't help the dread music playing in his mind like in the old movies when something terrible was going to happen. Robin was the owner of the salon, and his boss. Of course she'd have something to say to him about his disappearing act today. Might as well face up to it like a man. He headed to the back of the salon and knocked on her office door.

"Come in."

He pushed the door open and immediately began apologizing. "Robin, I'm sorry I left the salon in a lurch this afternoon, and Melinda told me the trouble I caused her today, but I felt like I was doing the right thing going to the hospital with my client who got injured just outside, after her appointment."

Robin was giving him a dubious look from her seated position behind her desk, and when he finished speaking, she let out a huge breath. She motioned to the chair in front of her desk, and he sat. "Dax, why do you and I keep having this same conversation?"

He shook his head. "We've never had this conversation, Robin. I've never had a client slammed into by a bike rider right outside our salon after a massage. She had a concussion, by the way. She's still under doctor's orders. What did you want me to do?"

"Okay. We've never had this particular conversation before, you're right. But we've had so many similar ones, all with the same outcome. Like when you encountered a homeless person on the sidewalk on your way to work, and you felt compelled to take them for a hot breakfast in the diner. Making you late to work, and late for your first appointment."

"I didn't want to just give her the money. I wanted to actually make sure she got the nourishment of eating a hot …"

"Or how about the time there was a puppy with a broken leg outside your apartment and you took him to the vet clinic instead of coming to work?"

He gasped. "He'd just been hit by a car, Robin. What was I supposed to do? Leave him there?"

"You have a Superman complex."

"Excuse me?"

"You feel compelled to rescue anyone or anything you come into contact with. Although it's admirable, don't get me wrong, it's disruptive. To your job. My salon. Every time you're unexpectedly late, I have to pick up the pieces. Or someone I pay, has to pick up your pieces. Just like Melinda did all day today. Scrambling around, getting replacements for you, calling your clients. No. This ends now. I expect you to come to work when you're scheduled. Period. And work your shift, and *then* go home. Got it?"

He rubbed his hand over his eyes.

"I'm afraid I'm going to have to take disciplinary action, Dax. I'm going to dock one dollar an hour from your pay until I see improvement for one month."

He needed to think. He'd never reacted well to threats, especially when they didn't seem to be in his best interests.

He could see her point, but why couldn't she see his? What she was calling a Superman complex, he called being a decent human being. Helping others in need. Isn't that what Jesus called them all to do, in the Bible? He wasn't a biblical scholar, but he was sure that was the gist of Jesus' teachings. *Do unto others as you would have them do to you.* Or was that the Golden Rule? He was never sure. Or how about this one? *What you have done to the least of my brothers, you have done for me.* He was quite certain that one was biblical. New Testament — one of Jesus's teachings.

So, the question is, did he want to work in a place that was forcing him to go against Jesus's teachings? Go against trying to live his life like a good person would?

What would he be giving up if he left this place? A paycheck, sure. But they weren't paying him much, and now, even less. Considering he had to pay for all his supplies — his massage table, his stereo to play soothing music, his oils, his uniforms. Not to mention, he still had a large student loan payment to pay off that debt for his training. And under his current pay, he was barely making a dent in that.

As he thought it over, the answer was clear. This wasn't a good place to spend his days, *even though* they were paying him to do the job he wanted to do. It seemed backward to quit, but not when he looked at the full picture.

He didn't have a parent to run this decision by, and he wasn't what he would consider a full-fledged Christian yet — he was working on it, but not quite yet. But he took a moment to pray to God for guidance in this decision. A quick, silent, fleeting *Guide me, Father.* He didn't know if it would make any difference, but at least by shooting the request up there to the Father, he'd feel a little more confident about his decision than if he just made it alone.

He opened his eyes and looked directly at Robin, who was watching him smugly. "I want to thank you for the opportunity you've given me these last few months. And apologize for the trouble I've caused you, too. But Robin, I can't work somewhere that doesn't support me in my efforts to help others. So, I quit."

It was obvious she hadn't expected that. She leaned forward so quickly she almost fell out of her chair. She sputtered, "That's not, no, no, that's not necessary. I wasn't saying that, Dax."

"My decision," he affirmed.

"Dax, think about this. You've got a paying job in your field. Why would you give that up? You're gaining valuable experience."

He shrugged. "You're not paying me enough to even make ends meet outside my expenses. Now you're threatening to dock my pay to discipline me. I think I can do better."

She frowned. "You were due for a raise consideration in four months ..."

"Which you would probably deny, am I right, because you consider me a performance problem."

The fact that she didn't deny it meant that he was right. His heart was lighter than it had been in months. This was the right decision.

"I'll gather my stuff and go. Can I contact my regular clients and let them know where I land?"

"Absolutely not. Those clients aren't yours, they're clients of this salon."

Okay. He was on his own. Again.

Chapter Five

Jasmine sighed at the sight of herself in the mirror. The bruises on her face had become a multi-color rainbow — blue, purple, an ugly tannish color — covering whatever centimeter of skin that wasn't covered by the gauze bandage on her forehead. Her eyelids even sported the colors. She couldn't help but cringe when she saw it. How would others who didn't know her react?

Putting herself on display at the restaurant tonight and at the graduation ceremony tomorrow evening would make her feel like a freak show. She glanced at her makeup collection, wondering if it was even worth the effort to try to cover it up.

She'd just picked up the small bottle of foundation when her mom walked in. Her expression changed when she took in the scene.

"Are you feeling up to going out to dinner? I could just as easily make something for you here."

Jasmine shrugged. "I don't want this face to stop me from enjoying my graduation weekend, you know? I'll never have another one." She put on a pouty-faced frown. "Stupid bruises."

Leslie took the makeup from her hand and placed it back on her vanity. "If you got it, flaunt it. You're not going to hide that color, you might as well not try."

"Everyone's going to look at me. And what about pictures with the family tomorrow? I'll be forevermore documented in the family annals with these awful bruises."

Leslie smiled. "Think of it this way. If you end up having sons, they'll think their mom is super-cool for having such awesome bruises."

Jasmine laughed. "Really?"

Leslie nodded. "Jasmine, you are a beautiful young lady, no matter if you have bruises and bandages on your face or not. I'm proud of you for working so hard at college and finishing your degree. I couldn't care less what you look like, and you shouldn't either. As long as you're physically feeling up to it — let's keep our plans the same. What do you say?"

Jasmine agreed. This stupid accident wouldn't ruin her graduation celebration. She wouldn't let it.

Hank, Leslie and Jasmine rode to Maxie's Supper Club later that evening. Her dad was already there, waiting, and standing beside him in the foyer was Dax. She gave him an appreciative stare. Brown dress pants hugged his long legs. A casual tweed sports jacket covered a white button down shirt, open at the neck. With his wavy brown hair brushing over the top of his collar, and the casual scruff of whisker covering his jaw, he could've easily been a male model waiting for his turn at the cover of GQ. She should know. She worked in that field, after all.

Or, wanted to, now that she was graduating.

She tried to ignore the stress that formed in her esophagus every time she thought about her job search — or lack thereof. What if all the entry-level jobs in the fashion industry were snatched up by more industrious and on-the-ball fashion majors than her? By waiting on her job search till after graduation, what if she was left with opportunities like working retail at a TJ Maxx?

She pushed the negativity away, painted her normal smile on her face, and went to greet her father with a kiss on the cheek, then turned to Dax.

"Hi," she said and couldn't help but notice that her voice had a breathy tone to it. Would he guess she was so happy to see him because of how absolutely hot he looked standing there?

"Hi," he responded and took both her hands in his. He leaned in to kiss her cheek and as he planted his lips there, she inhaled his wonderful scent. Nothing overpowering, but she could picture him spraying some manly cologne on himself, and it was flattering to think that he'd most likely done that with her on his mind. Well, he wouldn't have done it for her two fathers or her mother, would he?

"You smell good," she whispered in his ear, and at her words, he squeezed her hands and pulled back from her, a breathtaking smile on his face.

"You do, too," he said, his voice a tad husky.

She was so focused on him that she almost missed her mother studying the two of them, turning to Hank and saying something softly to him. Hank turned to watch them too, laughed and nodded. Fine, let them think whatever. Part of celebrating her graduation was sharing a dinner with this handsome man. She'd never see him again after tomorrow, so she was going to enjoy every second.

Until his next words. "Your face looks painful. Is it?"

Oh, Lord. She'd totally forgotten what a monster she looked like to others, including her handsome dinner date. Her hands flew up to her complexion, as if to hide the discoloration. "Um, only when something touches the bruising. I took a nap earlier and even the pillow caused some discomfort."

He took her hands and pulled them away. "Then don't touch your face. I don't want you in any more pain than you have to be."

The good thing about looking like a hideous monster was that he now felt it was his duty to hold her hands. "I'm sorry I look so hideous."

"You don't," he said, shaking his head. "You look gorgeous in that dress, and the bruises are temporary. I just thank God you had no fractures or permanent injuries. You'll be good as new soon."

The host led them to their table of five. Jasmine sat first, Dax beside her, then her dad placed himself on her other side, leaving Mom and Hank to take the two seats furthest away from her. Nobody caused a scene. It was customary for the Malones to be civil and well-mannered, and besides, Mom had been with her all afternoon, so it was Dad's turn to be near her.

Dinner itself was delicious, conversation was adequate, although a little strained, and afterward, Jasmine convinced her mom that she and Hank should go check into their hotel and allow Dax to deliver her back to her apartment. Leslie and Hank had been on Jasmine-duty ever since hitting town after their long drive. It was time for them to go settle in to their room for the night and get rested for the day of graduation festivities tomorrow.

She kissed all three of her parents good night, thanked them all for coming, and for the wonderful dinner. Dax shook hands with the men and leaned down to her petite mom and planted a polite kiss on her cheek, thanking them all for inviting him.

Then, they headed back to his car. It was an old one, some late model American boat, but it had personality. He opened the door for her and she slid on to the wide seat, watching him close the door and walk around to his side. When he got in and started the engine, she said, "Thank you for coming to dinner. I think it was easier for my mom and dad with a guest there. It put them both on their best behavior."

He laughed. "I don't know your parents well, but I can't imagine they would've gotten in a Jerry Springer brawl if I hadn't shown up."

She grinned. "No, but with Hank there, my dad might've felt outnumbered. Uncomfortable. I don't know. I just feel like the dynamic was better with you there."

"My pleasure," he said. He turned so he was facing her, and despite the darkness in the parking lot, in the car, she knew exactly when he leaned in close, took her chin impossibly gently in his hand and placed his lips on hers. Her heart rate increased a hundredfold and she gasped softly and closed her eyes.

He pulled away and she popped her eyes open to see his wide. "Did I hurt you?"

Confusion at his question quieted her, and then she remembered. "No. No, not at all." *Kiss me again, you fool.*

He leaned in as slowly as before and placed his lips on hers again. Nothing hard, nothing fast, just a sweet brush of his soft lips over hers. He inhaled and brought a finger up to her hair, pushing it behind her ear, being careful not to touch any of her bruising, anywhere that might cause an ounce of discomfort.

It was the most peaceful and yet heart-racing kiss she'd ever experienced.

The care he was taking with her made a rush of emotion flood her heart. And all too soon, it was over. He pulled back from her, keeping his eyes on hers as he settled back into the driver's seat. He ran a hand over his lips, took a deep breath and put the gear shift in reverse and backed the boat up.

"You're so beautiful, Jasmine."

"So are you." It had come out without thought. Sure, she thought he was, but that probably wasn't the best response. She laughed. "I mean, thank you, and you're very handsome as well."

He chuckled.

"In fact," she went on, "have you ever done any modeling?"

He flashed her a dubious look and shook his head. "No."

"You should! You have the right build. Tall and slim. You make clothes look good."

He stayed quiet, but his face tinged a little pink. She'd embarrassed him. "Seriously, that's what designers look for. People who wear clothes well."

He shook his head with a smile. "I've never thought of modeling before. I'm busy enough trying to get my massage therapy career up and running."

She let her memory wander to the hour she'd spent under his magic hands earlier today. "You've got a real gift for that, too. See, you're a man of many talents."

They pulled into her apartment parking lot and walked together to her door. "Thank you again for the dinner invitation," he said. "I enjoyed your family."

"Really? I mean, I love them like crazy, but they're mine."

"Do you have any other family members?" he asked.

"A few. A couple cousins, an aunt and an uncle. And now that Mom married Hank, I have his family members too. A growing list of stepbrother, stepsisters, and in-laws. It's pretty cool, actually. Oh! And a step-niece — an adorable little girl named Stella, five years old."

He nodded with a smile.

"How about you? What's your family like? Do they live here in town?" She watched his face transform from casual and happy, to something else. Something sadder. Had she stepped into an undesirable topic? "Oh, I'm sorry, I ..."

"No, it's okay. I'll tell you. But it's not a conversation to have while standing outside your door. Do you mind if we go in?"

She dug through her big purse for her keys and opened the door. He walked in first and looked around. It was a typical off-campus college student apartment, nothing to get too attached to, nothing she'd put too much energy into decorating. But suddenly, she wanted him to like it. "Make yourself comfortable. Would you like anything?"

He shook his head. "No. No, thanks."

He settled into her couch and leaned back, one long leg bent at the knee and resting over the other. "So, my family."

"Yes." She smiled and sat beside him, shifting so she faced him.

"I don't have any family."

He said it matter of factly, but the reality of his words was shocking. She knew her eyes popped open wide. "None?"

"No. Although my parents were married when they had me, it wasn't the first marriage for either of them, and they had other kids before me. Making them my half-siblings. Anyway, when I was born, it was a rocky time in their marriage. They stayed together for four more years, but during that time, it must've been hard to deal with an additional kid. So they passed me around to relatives. Aunts, uncles, family friends. They would each get me for six months or so, then they'd pass me on."

Jasmine frowned. His first four years, he was passed around from family member to family member? She remembered enough from her child psychology class to know that the first four years in a child's life were when the baby's character, self-esteem, and knowledge of right and wrong were established. What if a baby never had the same face to gaze up into during that time?

"Finally, when I was not quite five, they'd had enough. My mother and my father decided to split up, and they put me up for adoption."

"What? At the age of five?"

"Not quite five, but almost. I had my fifth birthday in a group home with about twenty other kids."

She grimaced. "And they just left you there?"

"Yep. Never saw or heard from them again."

She shook her head, unable to imagine it. "What about all those relatives who had taken care of you? Didn't they want to adopt you?"

His expression froze and he went speechless.

"I'm sorry …," she said, touching his arm. She hadn't meant to hurt him or insinuate anything. She was just trying to figure it out.

"Nope. I don't know the full story. I mean, I was four, you know? I still had my parents' last name, and that was it. It didn't take long before I forgot them altogether. My life was now the group home for orphans, and then, I started being assigned into foster care. I stayed with one family for nine months. That was my longest stay. Other than that, it was a few months in one place before moving to the next one."

Her head was spinning. His childhood had been so different than hers. She could barely relate to what he'd been through, so she focused on her outrage at his parents for putting him through it.

"Do you ever feel like doing a search? Finding your birth parents? Giving them a piece of your mind?"

"No. No way. Not for one second."

"Why?"

"Why would I? They obviously didn't want me then. I don't want them, now."

Jasmine nodded. She could understand. Good for him. He was on his own in the world, completely on his own. He had beaten the odds, grown up, got educated, was supporting himself. But was he lonely? She couldn't imagine life without family.

She moved her hand to his, and gripped it. He looked up, his locks falling away from his face as he did. "I'm sorry," she whispered.

There was so much about him she didn't know. How had he survived such a dubious upbringing? Had he been a wild child? Did he have abandonment issues?

He actually put a smile on his face and said, "Don't be. I didn't tell you that to make you feel sorry for me." He laughed. "Although that may be a strategy to make you like me. The sympathy factor?"

She rested her gaze directly on his. He didn't need to do anything special to get her to like him. Despite only knowing him for one day, she'd landed on that realization herself. She liked him. "No."

"Okay," he said with a smile. "Look, I'm not sure why I told you all that. I usually don't offer it up. If people ask me about my family I usually just brush it off. I guess I wanted to confide in you becauseyou've got this openness, this friendliness. You seem trustworthy and easy to talk to."

She smiled. She liked hearing his perceptions of her.

"So, when you think you've got family problems, and one of your parents is driving you crazy, just stop and think that most people with no parents would give anything to have even one. Kind of puts things in perspective, you know?"

She gave a slow nod. "Wow, you're right. Even my dad, who made bad choices and broke my mom's heart."

"All people make mistakes. It's human nature. God forgives us for them, through His son who paid the ultimate price for our sins." He stopped quickly and gazed up at her.

"You're a Christian?" she asked. To look at him and hear his story, that would be the furthest guess from her mind.

"I'm trying," he replied cautiously.

"What do you mean?"

"I'm reading the Bible and I'm trying to get into prayer. It wasn't something I had growing up, but I'd like to give it a try now that I'm an adult."

Jasmine nodded, seeing him in a whole new light. She'd been raised in the church. Of course, she had parents, in particular, a mother who had taken her there every week. Her mom had set the example, and Jasmine didn't think anything of it. It was just their routine. And while she was there, she met great people, learned how to sing and talk about Jesus, and learned the right way to live. Although she'd engaged in her fair share of bad behavior, she'd never strayed too far from the Christian principles that were ingrained in her.

But looking at Dax, she had to wonder. Erase her mom from her life — would she seek out church? Seek out the Bible and prayer? The fact that he was *trying*, as he put it, without any guidance or adult leadership whatsoever, made her admire him even more. "That's wonderful, Dax."

His face flooded with a relieved expression.

"I'm a Christian too."

"Then I'm sure I have a million questions for you. Stuff I jot down that I'm not sure of, when I'm reading the Bible. Stuff I hear in the news and wonder about the Christian view. As I said, I'm just starting out."

She smiled, shaking her head. "There's never been a day that I haven't believed in Jesus. However, I don't have any answers for you. It's not about knowing the answers, or taking a test. It's about believing. And living your life in a way that Jesus is reflected. I don't go overboard. I mean, I'm not overly demonstrative about it. But I believe."

"Could we talk about it sometime?"

Sometime. The open-ended question made her think that maybe he wanted their friendship to go further than just this weekend. Or, maybe that was just wishful thinking. Maybe it had just slipped his mind that in about thirty-six hours, she was leaving New York for good.

"Sure."

He rose to his feet. "But not tonight. You must be exhausted. You need to get to bed and wake refreshed for your graduation day tomorrow. Do you need anything from me before I go?"

She came slowly to her feet. *Another one of your kisses would be good.* She could've said it. She was such a flirt, she *would've* said it to anyone else. Anyone she wasn't interested in, just to make them laugh or feel good. But it was different with him. If she said something like that, even though it was exactly what was on her mind, she'd make herself vulnerable. She'd put herself out there, and risk him knowing exactly what she was thinking.

And she couldn't remember the last time she'd felt that way about anyone.

So, she just walked him to the door, thanked him for the conversation and said goodnight.

* * *

The next day, her face hurt.

She'd slept through the night, so she hadn't kept up with the pain pills every four hours. A whole night lying on her cheek had caused her right one to swell. She rose slowly to a sitting position, then standing, made her way to the kitchen. Her cell phone rang while she was swallowing the big pill.

"How are you feeling this morning? Happy graduation day, by the way," her mom said.

She groaned. "Mommy, my face hurts," she wailed.

"I'll be right over," and her mom broke the connection. Not fifteen minutes later, Leslie was ringing her doorbell.

Jasmine spent the day with padded ice packs on her face, keeping up with the pill schedule, watching her mom pack her apartment belongings into boxes and suitcases and feeling so blessed to have her there. At four thirty, she put on her dress and shoes, and took another peek at the makeup collection in her bathroom. She'd be careful not to press, but she'd have to apply some. The fewer stares she drew due to the hideousness of her bruises, the better.

About twenty minutes later, she emerged.

"Wow, you can barely tell," her mom exclaimed.

She chuckled. She was just being nice, but even Jasmine had to admit, it was an improvement. They made quick plans, settled on a meeting spot after the ceremony, and Jasmine headed off.

The ceremony flew by. Not unlike how four years of college had flown by. People had told Jasmine when she was selecting a college, "These will be the best four years of your life." And they absolutely were. She'd matured from a child to a young adult. She'd learned how to work hard, to discipline herself, to make her own decisions. It was difficult not to get teary-eyed when she hugged friends who, in a lot of cases, she would probably never see again. Except for a handful of close friends in her fashion marketing program who she would stay connected with, her classmates would disperse on the world and go make it happen for themselves. Life was changing. Quickly.

She met up with her parents and Dax after the ceremony. Her mom pulled out a camera. Jasmine cringed internally. She put up with photos with all the combinations — her, Mom and Hank. Her and Dad. Her and Dax. Her and Mom.

After the ceremony was a reception where she introduced everyone to her favorite professors and friends. Then on to another restaurant dinner. The whole thing felt surreal. She was breezing through her final day as a college student. Her final day on campus. Her final day in Ithaca, NY. From now on, she wouldn't live here. Probably wouldn't even come here except for alumni events.

Wow, she was an alumnus. Unbelievable.

Her thoughts turned to what came next. "So guys, where am I going tomorrow?"

Her parents all looked up and began talking at once. Jasmine laughed. They were all inviting her to come stay with them. Which, she supposed, was better than having no invitations at all.

"It probably doesn't surprise you, knowing me as you all do, that my plans extended no further than my graduation ceremony tonight. Now that that's done, and I have two 'homes' to choose from, I have no idea where to go now."

Leslie said with a smile, "The beach is awfully pretty this time of year."

Tim said, "She's not going for a vacation, Leslie. She needs to start looking for a job. Pittsburgh is a better place for that than a little sleepy beach town."

Leslie's shoulders tensed, and Hank's hand unhesitatingly came up and began a quiet massage. "What's wrong with a short vacation before she starts the work of her job search? Besides, she can write resumes and send emails from Pawleys just as well as Pittsburgh."

"Do you even have wifi?" he asked.

"Of course we do."

Jasmine made a Timeout sign with her hands. "Whoa, folks. I'll make sure I spend time in both locations this summer. While I'm looking for a job, I'll spend time in Pittsburgh and Pawleys. But I guess I'm feeling like I'll start at Dad's place. He can help me get the job search kicked off, then I'll go spend a week or two at the beach to relax while I'm waiting for interviews. That sound good?" She swung her head from her dad to her mom, and neither of them objected.

"Okay."

Dax cleared his throat. "What time do you plan to leave?"

Jasmine shrugged. "No specific time. Mom did most of my packing today. It's not that long a drive to Pittsburgh. Mid-morning?"

"How about I come over about nine and load the car for you?"

Her heart fluttered at his suggestion and she couldn't think of a single reason to decline it. So she smiled and agreed.

* * *

Graduation was over. College was done. Parents were happily farewelled. The apartment was packed. Two cups of coffee from her recent run to her favorite shop sat on her counter. All that stood between putting her student days permanently behind her, and facing her future as a (hopefully soon) working adult, was seeing Dax one more time.

Her doorbell rang exactly on schedule, its buzz echoing through the now empty apartment. She pulled the door open and the smile that formed on her face at the sight of him was one of joy. And from her vantage point, it sure seemed like the one he returned was just as joyful.

Before she chickened out, she stood on her tiptoes, reached for his face and rested her lips on his. She had no idea why. It seemed like a good idea.

He tipped his head when she ended the kiss and laughed. "Good way to start the day."

She stepped back and motioned him in. "I got you coffee." She led him back to the kitchen.

"Even better." He took a sip as he closed his eyes. Jasmine decided she liked guys who enjoyed things so much that they closed their eyes to savor it. Like coffee. And kissing.

He set the cup down. "Looks pretty empty around here."

"Yeah, my parents all helped last night. It was a little awkward." She shut up quickly and looked at him. "Not complaining!"

He laughed. "You don't have to censor yourself around me. I notice people with parents tend to joke about what a pain they are. But it's good-hearted, I'm sure."

"Yeah. It was just weird, you know? With the divorce and all."

He nodded. "There were a few tense moments, but all in all, I'd say they did pretty well. When's the next time they'll all be together?"

Jasmine thought about it, her eyebrows moving up into her bangs. "I can't imagine. My wedding, maybe?"

He laughed. "Okay. So, a while, then."

He looked so good. Shorts hugged his tanned legs, his feet in athletic sneakers and a tee-shirt casually thrown on. He was the epitome of casual, and yet, all those clothes seemed custom-made for him, like they couldn't possibly look better on anyone else. He could just as well be showing up for a photo shoot than to help her load her car.

"Let me load your car and then I'll finish the coffee."

She nodded and led him to her empty bedroom. All that remained were the furniture that came with the place, her suitcases, and whatever boxes her dad couldn't fit into his car when he left last night. He hoisted the biggest of the boxes and she admired the way his biceps bulged at the effort. She pulled the handle out of her suitcase and rolled it to the front door. He followed her to the parking lot and she unlocked her car.

They carried her belongings outside, and soon it all sat, surrounding her car. He studied the trunk and the back seat and then methodically inserted everything like it was a big jigsaw puzzle. It was one of those tasks that was uniquely male. Her dad had always packed the car for a roadtrip, never her mom. It was an innate talent, finding just the right combination to make best use of the limited space.

Closing the trunk, he rubbed his hands together and smiled at her. "There. You should be good to go."

"Thanks," she breathed, then remembered. "Don't forget your coffee."

"Ahhh." He followed her back upstairs for the last time. She wrangled her key off her key ring and placed it on the counter, as her landlord had asked her. The place sparkled like it never had while she was living there, and smelled of the Clorox her mom had cleaned it with last night.

She took a deep breath and let it out. She turned to him. He'd been watching her, holding his tongue. She shrugged and stuffed her hands into her pockets. Might as well go for honesty.

"I wish I'd met you more than three days ago." Darn those tears welling up in her eyes. What would he think of her sentimentality?

"Me, too." He brought a gentle hand up to her face and used a thumb to brush her cheeks, then trail down to her chin. Then he looked closer. "Your bruises look better today. You heal well."

She broke out in a laugh. He did, too.

"Look," he said, "I've been thinking about how to say this. I'd like to stay in touch with you. If you're game. I know that sounds crazy. You've made a lot of friends here in your four years. I came in at the tail end. But I …"

What? She wondered. You …

"I like you."

Her words rushed out on a beaming smile. "I like you, too."

He studied her eyes, his own lips moving into a smile. "Really?"

"Yes." Who knows what they'd be like if they had more time together? Why couldn't they have met a year ago? Two? Three? But regardless, they did meet, and now neither of them wanted it to end. Maybe instead of being part of her student life, Dax would somehow become part of her post-college life.

God knew what He was doing. She just had to trust that.

He pulled out his cell phone and handed it to her. She went to his Contacts and entered her number. Then she retrieved her own cell from her purse and gave it to him. He did the same.

"Call me," she said. "Or text me. Friend me on Facebook. Send me a Private Message. Or a Tweet. Or a pic on Instragram." She laughed. "The opportunities are endless."

"But no texting and driving."

"Absolutely not."

He leaned in and this time, the kiss started gentle and careful, and moved into passion. He buried his hands in her hair, and she was starting to debate delaying her trip when he pulled away. "Drive safe."

"Okay," she breathed, feeling a little dizzy.

He lifted his coffee cup. "Thanks for the coffee."

"Don't mention it." Her heart rate returning to normal, she let him walk her to the door. Standing in the doorway, she stopped and turned, looked back, remembering the fun experiences, and yes, some heartache too, that had occurred in this apartment. College days were ending, the end of an era.

But boy, the future was looking exciting too. She said a quick *thank You* to God in her head, and walked into the next step of her life.

Chapter Six

"Dear Applicant, thank you for your application and resume for employment. Unfortunately, your skills do not fit our needs at this time."

Jasmine let out an exasperated sigh and hit Delete in her email Inbox for the fifth straight time. Strike-out, strike-out, strike-out. Nobody in the New York fashion industry wanted her. No one. Her first five submissions in her job search had resulted in a big fat "No thanks." Why? What was wrong with her? What was she lacking, that they wouldn't even give her a chance to prove herself? She came from a reputable school, had the right major, good grades and a very prestigious internship. Why wouldn't they even take a look?

Her dad walked into her room and leaned in the doorway. She looked over at him, her lip pouting and brow furrowed. "What?" he asked.

"Why does no one want me?" she wailed.

He walked in and sat on her bed. "How bad do you want it?"

She scoffed. "Very bad! Obviously. I went to college and studied this stuff for four years. I worked my butt off and spent a slave-labor summer in Paris working in the fashion industry. I know I could do this stuff, but they're not giving me a chance."

"Sweetheart, thousands of college graduates all over the world can say this same thing. What sets you apart? How hard are you willing to work? How many rejections are you willing to take to get to that first 'yes?' No one's going to hand you a career on a silver platter. You've got to earn it. Now, are you going to give up before you even really get started?"

She sighed. Adulthood was hard. Her life had always just sort tripped along. Happy childhood, great parents, good schools, solid friendships. A little bit of heartache, but not much. Now, this. Rejection. Having to prove herself. Working to make a mark in the world. "I guess I sound like a spoiled brat, don't I?"

He smiled and reached over to caress her hand. "I know you better than that. You are going to do this, Jasmine. You are going to get a job in the fashion industry and you are going to build a career doing what you love. And you're going to be successful. But! It's not going to happen all at once. And it's not going to be easy." He stood up. "Persevere, dear. Anything worth achieving is going to take work, rejection, adjustments and finally, success."

She sniffed. "How long till we get to the success part?"

He laughed, waved and left her room. She was kidding, of course, but not really. She wanted to skip over the hard stuff, and get right to the reward. But she guessed it wasn't going to happen that way. Fine. She'd suck it up and go through the steps.

* * *

"Dear Ms. Malone, we appreciate your interest in employment with our company. To be eligible for further consideration, please submit a fashion photo portfolio, featuring at least a half dozen original designs."

"Please submit a video featuring runway models wearing your design."

"Please submit a video of yourself expanding on where you see yourself in the fashion industry, both now, and in five years' time."

Jasmine exploded with a scream, took the handful of emails she'd printed out from perspective employers, and threw them in the air, watching them cascade down around her. The latest batch of emails from her job search were trickling in. Although they weren't rejections, they weren't job offers either.

Her dad appeared in her doorway, his tie loose around his neck. "What's the matter?" His voice was calm but she caught the trace of panic in his eyes.

She pointed to the white papers spread around her. "They all want something different. They all want the world!"

He studied her for a moment, then her meaning seemed to sink in. He took a few steps into the bedroom, and crouched down to pick up the discarded pages. He read them each with a frown, then looked up at her. "You could look at the bright side. They could've rejected you outright. The fact that they're asking for more means that you're still in the running. You're competitive." He handed the papers, now organized in a neat stack, calmly to her.

"Or they could've just extended a job offer. That would've been the brightest side."

He smirked. "Don't forget: step by step. Hard work, rejection, adjustments, and finally, success. You're moving from rejection to interest. What did you do to make that happen?"

She considered for a second. "I searched the fashion industry websites, refined and perfected my resume. I called and talked to some of my classmates to find out what they were doing that I could try."

He nodded his approval. "Good. You're doing the work. Building a career is worth the effort."

She quieted. He had a point. But why were her friends who graduated in engineering, computer science and actuarial, all posting on social media that they'd gotten jobs already? Nobody required them to do any extra work to be competitive. They just coughed up a job offer with a lot of numbers following the dollar sign. Why was the fashion industry so different?

"I guess you're right. But seriously? This stuff is going to take some time."

"You've got nothing but time right now. Your job search is your full-time job. Work at it eight, ten hours a day like you would a job, and you'll develop this stuff before you know it." He pointed at the papers. "You do, uh, have some original designs, don't you?"

She puffed out a breath. "If I can find them. I had to draw original designs for my Senior Seminar class, then actually sew the garments. I've got at least ten of them. Somewhere." They were in boxes packed from the apartment. But had those particular boxes ended up in Pawleys Island, or here in Pittsburgh? She had no idea.

He smiled a tight closed-mouth smile. "The presentation of them — the videos, the photos — they're an exercise in creativity. Which fortunately, you're really good at. Take your time, brainstorm, consult with friends, then put something together. Once it's all polished up, you can submit them.

That's how you stand out from the others, sweetheart. That's your ace in the hole. I have faith in you."

She sniffed. Dad: the all-business, smart-as-all-get-out parent. She could always count on him to raise the bar high and expect the world. Her whole childhood had been like that. He was a doctor, for goodness sake. How much more demanding could his career be? He'd set a solid example for her — both her parents had — of working hard to build a career that you loved. He was being supportive, encouraging, but not giving her any excuses to slack off.

"I can't really expect any sympathy from you, can I, Dad? Not a bit?"

He chuckled. "Sympathy is overrated. Hard work and determination is what gets results."

"Okay. I'll take a deep breath to keep from hyperventilating, and get to work. One at a time, take the time to do it right."

"That's my girl." He lifted his hands to finish tying his tie without even looking in a mirror. "I've got a hospital fund-raiser tonight, so I won't be home till late. I had the ladies stock the fridge and freezer so help yourself." He winked at her and left. She heard his voice as he walked down the hall. "Work hard and don't freak out!"

She laughed at his choice of words. Maybe raising a daughter had taught him a few things after all.

Suddenly, he was back in the doorway. "I was just thinking — do you need any equipment? A good camera? A video camera?"

"Oh. I assumed I'd use my phone. But maybe that's not high enough quality."

"I don't know. Look into what you need, but I was going to offer you — it's several years old — more than several, actually. But I have a pretty good camera and it has video on it. It's in a box in the guest bedroom closet. Feel free to look."

"Thanks, Daddy."

He left again. They were getting along fine, her and him. Despite what he'd done to Mom, he was her dad, and he was trying. Maybe Mom wasn't ready to forgive him yet, but she supposed she was. Kind of a passive forgiveness while avoiding talking to him about it. Because it wasn't her business, was it, the sorry state of her parents' marriage. Talk about awkward. That conversation would definitely fall into the category of TMI.

She spent the next half hour researching the employers' websites to see if they required any particular type of film or video. Writing down the information she uncovered online, she wandered down the hall to the guest bedroom and opened the closet door. All that hung there were off-season coats and sweaters, and a few boxes on the high shelf.

She tugged at first one box, then the other, hoisting them off the shelf and onto the floor. Squatting down, she dug into the first box. It contained a variety of objects, all seemingly unrelated. Old loose photos from family vacations the three of them had taken when she was little. Copies of wedding photos, her dad young and handsome, her mom gorgeous and youthful in her long white gown.

Tears threatened and she scooped up all the wedding photos and set them aside. She refused to let herself become derailed by staring at the youthful, happy versions of her parents, deep into their eyes. Could she detect anything there? Could they possibly predict the outcome of their marriage? Twenty happy years, then, kaput?

No. The time to mourn her parents' marriage was not now. Still ..., she sighed. It sure was weird coming home from college and not having both of them there.

No camera here. But something odd caught her attention. In a bottom corner of a box was one of those accordion-style folders, an old brown container secured shut with an elastic band. She pulled it out and held it up to her nose. The musty smell of it was prevalent. Whatever it was, it had been here awhile.

Carefully, she unwrapped the elastic band, pushed it aside and opened the flap. She reached in and pulled out a handful of papers. A half dozen yellowed newspaper clippings and a few official-looking papers. She placed them on the carpet and scanned the clippings first. They were in chronological order, so she began to read.

They appeared to have been clipped from the Pittsburgh Post Gazette. Dateline: June 9, 1968. Headline: Infant Found, Abandoned in Phone Booth.

"This morning, an infant was delivered to Allegheny General Hospital. The infant was discovered lying in a basket placed on the floor of an enclosed phone booth on the corner of Penn and Fifth Avenues in Pittsburgh. The infant was female, in relatively good health, although slightly dehydrated, and upon examination by medical staff, is estimated to be approximately two days old. The infant is currently admitted to the newborn nursery at the hospital. The man who delivered her, who will remain unnamed, demonstrated full cooperation with hospital authorities, and is not considered a suspect of any wrongdoing at this time by Pittsburgh Police Department."

Jasmine frowned. What were these papers doing here? What relationship did they have to her family? Who had clipped them and why? One thing jumped out at her immediately. June 9 was two days after her mom's birthday of June 7. But 1968 — was that her mom's birth year? She paused to do some quick math in her head. If it wasn't exactly her birth year, it sure was close. That would make this baby 47 years old now. Isn't that about what Mom was?

She pulled out the next clipping and read. Dateline: June 10, 1968. Headline: City of Pittsburgh Wants to Help Phone Booth Baby.

"Public interest in our story run yesterday about a two-day old baby girl abandoned in a phone booth in downtown Pittsburgh and delivered to Allegheny General Hospital, ran very high. By noon yesterday the hospital had received over two hundred phone calls inquiring as to the health and status of the baby, and in addition, the newspaper had fielded a hundred calls. Pittsburgh police are investigating the abandonment and hospital officials are pursuing next steps with the city social services office. Due to public interest, a donation fund has been opened, and Pittsburgh residents with the desire to help the child can donate money, diapers, clothes or formula. Go to your local branch of Citizens Bank and make your donation. Once the fate of the baby is determined, all donations will go with her."

Jasmine flipped to the next clipping. A few days had gone by before another article was published. The next one was dated June 14. Headline: Fate of Phone Booth Baby Determined.

"Allegheny General Hospital officials, working with Pittsburgh Police and Pittsburgh Social Services, have decided to place the abandoned phone booth baby girl, previously reported on June 9 and June 10 into adoption eligibility through social services. Although public interest in adopting the healthy baby girl is high, Social Services announces that they will go through their normal processes for adoption. First priority will go to candidates who have previously completed the necessary paperwork and interviews, and been approved by the social services adoption authorities.

"Notice: as required by the social services process, the true parent(s) of this baby is hereby put on notice that they will have ten days to claim their baby, with proof of parenthood, before they relinquish their parental rights to the City of Pittsburgh."

The final newspaper clipping was a short one, not an article, but an entry in a listing of adoption notices. It read, "Baby girl, one month old, legally adopted by Ken and Adele Somers of Pittsburgh. Child is named Leslie."

Jasmine sat back on her heels, her mouth dropped open. Her mother was the Phone Booth Baby from 1968! She'd been somewhat of a minor celebrity in their city, to say the least. And someone had gone to the trouble to save this documentation about it. Her Grandma Adele, most likely.

She flipped through the rest of the papers in the accordion file: a police report from the original investigation. She scanned through it. Pretty routine, all the information showing up in the newspaper articles in some manner. All except ... the name of the Good Samaritan who found her mother, and took it upon himself to take her to the hospital where she would be in good hands. The paper had left his name out of it, maybe at his request. But he was one of God's helpers who had done the right thing. His name was Paul Mason. And that was all the information listed about him.

She closed her eyes and said a quick prayer of thanks to God for His servants on earth who carried out His work, people like this anonymous Paul Mason who found a baby girl in 1968 and took time out of his day to carry her to safety.

Next was the paper program from Leslie's baptism and christening ceremony in July, and finally, an old black and white snapshot of her mom as a beautiful baby in a flowing white gown, being held in the arms of both her Grandma Adele, who lived in Arizona now and her Grandpa Ken, who had died when Jasmine was just twelve.

Exhausted from her impromptu trip down memory lane, Jasmine laid back on the carpet and closed her eyes. Her mom — abandoned as a baby and adopted by Jasmine's grandparents. Why had she never heard this truth? A family secret that was never revealed? What the heck …?

Chapter Seven

The elementary school year hadn't ended yet in South Carolina, so Jasmine had to wait till at least 4:00 before she could call her mother. In the meantime, she searched the remaining boxes in the guest room, and located the camera Dad had referred to. It was a beauty. Probably top of the line the year he'd bought it, like everything else he bought. He'd probably gotten interested in photography as a hobby and tried it, before losing interest and storing the camera away in his closet.

She peered through the view finder and gave it a few sample clicks. He was right — it took some great digital photos and video. She wandered outside and took some close-ups of flowers, the mailbox, the condo, textures of brick and grass and wood. It would be a good tool in fulfilling her job search requirements. By late afternoon she had collected several hundred still shots and a dozen videos that she was happy with, and her abilities with the camera had moved beyond the novice stage.

When she placed the call to her mother's cell phone, she closed her eyes and pictured the beautiful location where her mother was. Pawleys Island, South Carolina was a tiny island off the coast of Myrtle Beach, the lifelong home of the Harrison family, now her family as well. Hank and his first wife had raised their family there — a son, Jeremy and a daughter, Marianne, who still were living their own lives there. Jasmine treasured her new siblings resulting from Mom's second marriage. And having the excuse for frequent trips to the beach now that school was over was just an added bonus.

There were plenty of places to stay, beachfront. Mom and Hank's huge oceanfront house on stilts, The Old Gray Barn. They got married there in a fun surprise wedding last fall that Hank had planned. As in Surprise! You're getting married in front of your friends and family, just eight months after your divorce. The man had guts, since he'd never officially asked her before he gathered all the important people in their lives together. He must've just been sure she'd say yes. And she did.

The Old Gray Barn had tons of bedrooms, and she knew she was always welcome there, and it had the added bonus of family history. As a child, Leslie, along with her parents and cousins and aunts and uncles used to gather there for family reunions at the beach.

If she wanted a change of scenery, or if she detected the need to give the newlyweds some privacy, she could always get a room at the Seaside Inn, a lovely beachfront inn run by Marianne and her husband, Tom. They not only ran it, they lived there with their daughter Stella. It was so homey and inviting with its big great room where guests gathered for socializing, the huge back porch where Marianne offered coffee and muffins every morning so guests could soak in the sun and the sound of ocean waves, and its delicious three meals a day served in the dining room, cooked by probably the best bunch of chefs of southern cooking in the entire state. At least, Jasmine thought they were, from what she'd tasted. Man, what those cooks could do with some shrimp, grits and cornbread.

"Hello?"

"Hey, Mom."

"Jasmine! Good to hear from you. Just getting ready to leave school."

"Are you doing a countdown yet?"

"Of course I am. Nine full school days left, plus a half day, and then, an hour."

Jasmine laughed. Her mom had taught school for over fifteen years, but she was just finishing her first year at Pawleys Island Elementary. Amazingly, she found kids on a small coastal island to be similar to kids in big-town Pittsburgh.

"How's the job search going?"

Jasmine sighed. "I have a lot of work to do. I have to make videos and take stills of people modeling my clothes."

"Wow."

"So, question for you. Did you bring boxes home from my apartment?"

"Yeah, a few."

"Would you mind looking through them? Somewhere I have about a dozen garments that I designed and made for Senior Seminar — original designs. I need to find the drawings and the garments themselves and see if I can use them for what these companies are asking me for."

"I'll do that as soon as I get home, and I'll call you back."

"Okay. And I also need to find models. Preferably a man and a woman, tall, slim, able to carry off clothes."

"Hmmm, at minimum budget, I assume."

"Budget? Who said anything about a budget? Free, of course."

Mom laughed. "Then you better start thinking about who from your high school crowd fits the bill and are still in Pittsburgh."

"Yeah." Jasmine shook her head. She was starting to feel that breathless/heart-racing thing at the thought of so much work to do. But the fashions weren't exactly the premiere topic on her mind to talk to Mom about. "But actually, Mom, I have another question for you."

"Yep."

"What do you know about the Phone Booth Baby?"

A moment of silence emerged from her phone, like a cloud of smoke emitting. Then, "The what?"

"The Phone Booth Baby. A certain baby girl was abandoned in a Pittsburgh phone booth back in 1968, discovered and taken to the hospital. The whole town fell in love with her story, donated a bunch of money and supplies, before she was finally adopted. By Ken and Adele Somers."

An uncomfortable laugh came over the line.

"Your parents, Mom. You were the Phone Booth Baby. And you never told me?"

"Sweetheart, I was an infant. Nothing to tell you about. I mean, do you have any memories of when you were a month old or less?"

"Of course not, but …"

"It's ancient family history. I hardly ever think of it myself. My entire life, I've been Ken and Adele's daughter. A Somers through and through, and then a Malone. And now a Harrison."

"It's so interesting, though."

"Honey, I'm sorry I never told you. It's no big deal."

"You seriously were never curious about your real parents?"

"Ken and Adele are my real parents."

"I know, I know, but your biological parents? Your mother, in particular? She gave birth to you, then two days later left you in a phone booth, hoping someone would find you. Can't you imagine what she must've been going through? What an internal battle she was fighting?"

Leslie paused. "No, seriously, honey. It's not even in my thought pattern."

"Did you *ever* think about it?"

"No. My parents were upfront with me about it. I think I was about six when they told me I was adopted. They told me about the phone booth and the abandonment, but they were so loving and gentle, they didn't let the news stir me. Make me feel unloved or in jeopardy. They just let me know that a lot of parents wanted to adopt me, but they were the lucky ones who got to take me home and keep me."

"Well, that's a great way to break the news to a child. But what about when you grew older? Weren't you curious? Didn't you want to dig into the mystery?"

She could hear her mom take a deep breath and let it out. "I think for my tenth birthday my mom gave me those clippings and documents that you must've found. She encouraged me to read them and ask her any questions I had. But I didn't care. I had a great family. I had a great childhood, a good life. I didn't want to be identified as 'The Phone Booth Baby.' It was evidently a novelty in the Pittsburgh news for a month or so, and then it passed. Why would I want to dig it all up again? Then or now?"

"Well, because maybe we could solve the mystery. We have the internet now, tons of resources that didn't exist back then. We could hire a private investigator. He could help us."

"Help us what?"

"Find your parents!"

Leslie exhaled. "I know exactly where my parents are. One's in Tucson and one's in heaven."

Jasmine frowned. Why did this have absolutely no importance to her mother? If Jasmine were the Phone Booth Baby, she'd be all over it, trying to solve this mystery. One last try to increase her mom's curiosity: "If this means nothing to you, why did you save this file after all these years?"

"I didn't. Not intentionally, anyway. When I cleared out the house after the divorce, I probably ran into the file and debated whether to pitch it or keep it. I tossed it in a box, which evidently ended up in your dad's condo."

A sigh of frustration crossed Jasmine's lips. This story had gripped her attention, her curiosity. She didn't have time to dig into it now. She had to get this job search going and give that her full focus. But she'd been hoping to get her mother on the job, now that her summer break was approaching. This felt important.

But Mom didn't think so.

"All right," she said, letting it go for now. "Say hi to Hank and Marianne and Jeremy for me. I'll plan a trip to the beach around the time you're off school."

"Love you, sweetheart."

* * *

"When can you start?"

Dax smiled. Turns out, it wasn't all that difficult to find work as a licensed massage therapist in a big town like Ithaca,

New York. His training and experience made him practically sought after.

"Tomorrow?"

His new boss, a man about ten years his senior named Roscoe, shook his hand. Dax had told Roscoe about his passion for volunteer work and asked for a smidge of flexibility when required. Roscoe not only agreed, but complimented on his commitment to helping others. Dax left the new salon, smiling and thinking a *Thank You* to God. Maybe he'd found his new place. Time would tell.

To celebrate, Dax got in his car and headed over to Jefferson School. It was only fifteen minutes before quitting time, and he knew of one particular seventh grader who would be glad for an unscheduled visit. Pedro had been his mentee for two years now, through a program set up by the school district. Dax had volunteered to work one-on-one with kids in the foster care system. He knew only too well what a difference a big-hearted adult could make in the development of young boys in need of a role model. Dax himself was lucky enough to have hooked up with a few men who had filled that father-role for him, at least temporarily. Navigating the treacherous waters through adolescence to manhood was difficult if you had no one to watch and learn from.

The program Dax was involved in allowed him to meet with Pedro regularly — once or twice a week after school, more time on weekends, if all parties were agreeable. Fortunately, Dax had hit it off well with not only Pedro, but his current foster mom, Darlene, whom Pedro had lived with for close to a year now. She was a kind-hearted woman, but tired more often than not, and appreciated when Dax could pick up the slack with Pedro.

Dax pulled out his phone and found Darlene in his Contacts, and gave her a quick call. "Darlene, it's Dax."

"Oh, hi."

"It's not my afternoon for Pedro, but I wondered if you had plans for him. I'm at his school now and have something to celebrate. I thought I could pick him up, take him for ice cream, work on homework, and have him back in time for dinner."

She laughed. "Sure, you know it. What are you celebrating?"

"New job."

"Oh. What was wrong with the old one?"

He smiled. "They just wouldn't let me be me."

She laughed. "You young folks. You don't know how good you have it." Darlene worked a full-time, and a part-time job, in addition to fostering to make her own ends meet.

He ended the call and before long, Pedro came out, absorbed in a crowd of pre-teen kids all jockeying for position. They splashed onto the sidewalk in front of the school like a tidal wave, then began to break apart and disband as some headed for the line of school buses, others for parents' cars, and still others walking down the sidewalk. Dax jumped out of his car and jogged over, wanting to catch Pedro's attention before he climbed onto his bus.

"Yo, Pedro!"

The boy's head whipped up and he saw him, a smile growing. "Yo, man!" he said and Dax pulled him into a quick hug — enough to show his affection, but not enough to embarrass the kid in front of his friends. "What are you doing here?"

"I had some good news to share and thought you'd be up for some ice cream to celebrate."

"Cool!" The kid was always up for ice cream. Or cake. Or burgers. Or anything edible. His stomach didn't seem to have a cut-off valve. "What's the good news? You getting married?"

Dax laughed as he put his arm on Pedro's shoulders and walked him over to the car. "No, that's not it."

"You got a girlfriend?" Pedro intoned it like he was teasing, drawing out the syllables and practically singing the word. Dax was well aware that at Pedro's age, the correct response was always denial, "No! I ain't got a girlfriend!" like that was the worst thing in the world. However, with age came maturity and clarity, and Dax knew that a relationship with a woman was something he wanted. Very much. And Pedro didn't know how close he was, since Dax was now convinced he'd met the woman of his dreams, and the few short hours he'd spent with her had been among the finest in recent memory.

Jasmine.

"What if I do?" Dax teased, and Pedro went crazy like a twelve-year-old would, pretend-gagging and carrying on like it was a punishment worse than death. "No, I'm just kidding, no girlfriend," Dax went on, knowing it was the truth. Sharing a few kisses and a few dinners with a girl who had just moved three hundred miles away, did not make a relationship qualify for girlfriend status. But on the other hand, he wouldn't qualify them as just friends either. He had a few friends, and he not once felt his heart race while holding hands, like it did with Jasmine.

Regardless, he wasn't about to jinx whatever fledgling relationship he had with the beautiful Jasmine by sharing a peep about it with Pedro. "I got a new job, buddy. This one pays me a little more, and hopefully will appreciate me a little more. By the way, I know it'll be a while till you work, but try to remember this."

"Yeah?"

"Make sure you work at a place that respects you and supports you."

"Okay."

"Your life will be miserable if you don't."

They got in the car and drove to a nearby ice cream place. It just happened to be Pedro's favorite place, one that he rarely got to visit unless Dax took him. And Dax didn't mind having that distinction at all.

They picked out their favorites: Dax an ice cream sundae topped with peanut butter and Pedro some awful-sounding concoction called The Kitchen Sink containing just about every ice cream topping he'd ever heard of, all combined onto four scoops of ice cream. There had to be at least a thousand calories in it, and God knew how many sugar grams.

"Just promise me you'll still eat your dinner later," he said to Pedro as they carried their treasures to the table. "Darlene knows you're here, but it would be rude not to eat the dinner she makes for you, because you're stuffed from ice cream."

Pedro gave him a dubious look, his forehead creasing and his eyes wide, looking up at him through his dark bangs.

Yeah, Dax knew. Stuffed from ice cream? Get real. Dax laughed and rumpled his hair, and they sat.

First came inhaling the ice cream. Then came talking about Pedro's day, then it was time for homework. Pedro pulled a few books out of his backpack and was just pointing out some Algebra problems that made absolutely no sense to him, when Dax's phone rang.

"Hello?"

"Hi Dax." Her voice made his heart stop, then rush to catch up.

"Jasmine." He glanced at Pedro. He planned to motion for him to work on his math while he took his phone call a few steps away, but the darn kid had heard the name he'd breathed, in what Dax was sure a tone Pedro had never heard him use before.

Pedro's attention was glued to Dax, and he immediately began making smooching sounds, and repeating, "Jasmine, oh hi, Jasmine, I love you, Jasmine!"

Dax tried a stern frown and shake of his head, but with his mood so happy that Jasmine had called, he couldn't quite pull it off.

"Who's that?" Jasmine's voice came over the phone.

Dax stood and pointed at Pedro, then his book, then turned his back to him. "That ... is Pedro."

"Why's he saying my name so much?"

Darn it. How could he be cool when a twelve-year-old Romeo was complicating things?

"Let me talk to her!" Pedro had followed him, was standing right beside him, and had ripped the phone out of his hand before Dax had a chance to object. "Hi, Jasmine?"

Dax couldn't hear Jasmine's side of the conversation but he tried to send Pedro a telepathic message not to say anything rude or inappropriate. Remember at least *some* of the lessons Dax had taught the kid over the last few years.

"Oh, well, congratulations on your graduation." Pedro was talking into the phone, his eyes locked with Dax's, and then he lifted his thumb and nodded his head with a smile. "He brought me here for some celebration ice cream. He got a new job. Um, let me see ..." he pulled the phone away. "Still a massage therapist, Dax?"

Dax nodded.

"Yes, still massage therapist. Um, they let him be him. At least more than the other place."

Dax sighed. Enough was enough. He held his hand up to Pedro, waggled his fingers at him.

"Okay, well, it was nice talking to you, but Dax wants the phone back now." The kid handed it back to him and murmured, "She sounds nice."

Dax put his hand over the phone. "Great, now go sit over there and do your homework and don't interrupt me again, you got it?"

Pedro nodded with a smile, his face looking like he wanted to say something, but he refrained and did as he was told.

Dax took a breath, let it out, and spoke into the phone. "Sorry about that. He's a good kid, but he gets a little curious sometimes."

Her laughter was warm. "How do you know him?"

"He's my mentee. I meet him after school a few days a week, talk to him, help him with homework, you know."

"That's sweet of you."

Dax shrugged, even though she couldn't see it. "I get as much out of it as he does. He's a lot of fun."

"I bet you're making a big difference with him."

"Hope so. Hey," he said, ready to change the subject, "so you're home. How was the trip? How's everything going?"

"Good, good." She started telling him about her job search, and how the employers she'd contacted now wanted her to submit this and that, and she was somewhat stressed out about the requests. But as much as he wanted to listen to the words she was saying, he found himself instead bathing in the timbre of her voice. It did intense things to his body. It made his heart race, his hands shake a little, his breathing unsteady.

Then she threw one on him. "Hey, I just had a great idea. Remember how I told you, you would be a great model because you have the right look for it?"

"Yeah." He did remember. He couldn't help but feel flattered when she'd said it.

"How would you like to help me with some of these employment projects? The video and the still photos? You could be my male model."

He chuckled, loving how enthused she seemed about the prospect. "You realize I have absolutely no experience at this, right?"

"That's all right! First of all, I can't pay a model with experience."

"I'm cheap, in other words."

"Exactly. And, I know a natural when I see it. I bet you look great on film."

A smile covered his face. Any excuse to see Jasmine again was good. Her seeking him out to help her because she thought he'd look great on film – that just had to be good.

"How about it?" she asked now. "Would you be able to make some time to come to Pittsburgh and help me by modeling some clothes while I photograph and videotape you?"

"I'd love to. As long as you realize that you'll need to show me what you want me to do."

"No problem." They made plans and set a date, far enough out that Jasmine would have time to design and sew his clothes, and that he would work at his new job a while before taking time off. They chatted about other things, and finally, with a smile on his face and anticipation in his heart, he said good-bye.

Chapter Eight

No rest for the weary. The cliché was etched in Jasmine's mind, and had been ever since her graduation. She'd dived into her job search, addressing her abundance of rejections, then into the designs and sewing required by her application projects. Good thing she enjoyed designing and sewing clothes, or she'd embody another cliché too: *All work and no play makes Jasmine a dull girl.*

But, she didn't feel like a dull girl today. In fact, today, she was a very excited girl. Because today she was expecting a visitor. A very handsome, sweet, generous visitor: Dax.

She'd decided that in order to prove her versatility to potential employers, she needed to demonstrate fashions for both men and women. Heck, she'd even try children's styles if she had to. She wanted a job in the fashion industry, and if it meant pushing herself out of her comfort zone and designing clothes that she'd never designed before, she'd do it.

For the last week, she focused on three diverse outfits for her male model to bring to life on film. A casual shorts, cotton shirt and hat combo. A dressier slacks and long-sleeve dress shirt, and then a formal dark suit. Yes, she'd actually made a suit on her sewing machine in her dad's spare bedroom. Keeping in mind that it only needed to look good on film. It didn't have to be as durable as a real suit. Just enough to transport her design ideas from pencil on paper, to fabric on a body.

Dax's body. With his long, lean legs, slim waist and perfect torso, she knew he'd look good in these clothes. The multitude of successful male models she'd worked with last year during her Paris internship had nothing on Dax. She just needed to make him comfortable enough to loosen up in front of the camera. Let him connect his eyes with the lens and make everyone fall in love with him.

She shook off her nerves and went upstairs to the spare bedroom. It would become Dax's room during the few days he was here. She double-checked the three new creations hanging in the closet. She'd washed them by hand, sprayed them with starch and pressed them with her steam iron. They were ready for their photo shoot. As soon as Dax arrived, they could begin.

Take a breath. She couldn't forget her manners. When he arrived, he may need a drink, a meal, a chance to stretch his legs. Then, the photo shoot. Her fingers were itching to get started.

The doorbell rang and her heart jumped. Her legs pumped down the stairs and she reached the front door breathless. She pulled it open.

It was, indeed, Dax. He'd thrown on a simple long-sleeved white shirt and it looked like it was born to grace his form. Long, worn jeans covered those legs that were going to convince fashion professionals that her own pants designs belonged on their payroll. She was happy to see he hadn't cut his hair. That long brown hair that flowed carelessly past his shirt collar, making her hands ache to reach out and run her fingers through it.

"Hi," he said with a smile and she realized she'd left him standing for several long beats while she simply stared, taking in the beauty of him.

"Hi," she laughed, reached for his hand and pulled him inside the condo. He laughed too, and what came next seemed natural. Unavoidable. She pushed up onto her tiptoes, craned her neck and kissed him. Their lips joined and she closed her eyes. Soft, moist lips on hers, her nostrils breathing in the scent of him, leather and wind. She barely knew him, but her lips knew his, and they felt like they belonged right there, together.

She pulled away. Conversation, yes, that's what was needed here. Because if she didn't engage her lips in speaking, they'd just want to keep busy attacking his with more kisses. "How was your trip? Are you hungry? Thirsty? Tired? Do you need anything?"

His eyebrows dipped at her. My gosh, she sounded so nervous. Because that's what this man did to her. She hadn't known a guy in a long, long time who so excited her that she was nervous and breathless around him. "Take two. Sorry. Come in, Dax. Have a seat. Would you like anything?"

He followed her into the living room and chuckled. "Great to see you."

She looked at him over her shoulder. "Yeah, you too."

They sat and he told her about his new job. He was working to build his clientele, and hoped that when his previous clients found out where he'd landed, they would bring their business to him. She told him about her designs and the outfits she'd sewn for him to wear.

"I want to see them."

She nodded. "Go get your stuff and we'll take it up to your room and I'll give you the tour."

He left and returned a moment later with a small duffle bag. They went up the stairs and into the spare bedroom. Jasmine made a circle in the middle of the room, arms out. "While you're here, this is your home base." She pointed out, "Bed, dresser, closet. Bathroom," she opened the door, "is a shared one between your room and mine. My room's on the other side." She closed the door and smiled. "But seriously, make yourself comfortable. Feel at home. I'm so glad you're here, helping me with this project." She smiled and bit her tongue on the rest of the sentence that she knew she shouldn't say aloud: and spending more time together will help me figure out how the heck I feel about you, and what could possibly come next in this, um, would you call it a relationship?

No. Definitely shouldn't tell him that.

"Wow. This is nicer than my room at home."

"Well, it's a new condo, and no one's ever stayed in this room before."

Dax was standing in the doorway of the closet, and reached out to finger the new suit. "Is this …? Did you make this?" He looked over at her, his features squished into amazement.

Her heart raced a little faster. "Well, yes, but remember it's not final quality. It's just supposed to look good on film. I mean, you wouldn't be able to wear it to work all day — it's not that durable. But you should be able to put it on and model it for the camera. I made it based on the measurements you gave me, but we'll tailor it to your body, make sure everything fits just right." She was rambling. Great.

He was staring at her, his eyes directly on hers, full of admiration. When she finally shut her mouth, he turned to her and took her arms with his hands. "You're amazing. You're so talented. You actually made this? A full men's suit? In the last week?"

She shrugged. "Well, yeah. I'm a designer and seamstress. It's what I do. Well, it's what I want to do."

"This is the kind of job you're applying for?"

She smiled. "Yeah."

"Well, all we have to do is make those guys in New York see what I see. Your talent, your innovation. You'll blow them all away. They'll be fighting over you." He pulled her into his arms and she nestled her head into his chest, breathing in that now familiar scent. She was becoming so comfortable here, in his arms, sharing her dreams and her ambitions with him. How had this happened so fast? He was now a part of her life. Exactly *what* part of her life, she didn't know. But maybe while he was here, they could figure it out together.

She pulled back and looked up at his beautiful face, his warm cocoa-colored eyes. "I'm so glad you're impressed. Together, we'll make some videos and still photos that we both believe in."

He nodded. "Here's an idea. Have you ever thought of asking God to lead you in your job search?"

"No. What do you mean?"

He cleared his throat, still holding loosely onto her hands. "Well, we know that all things are better if God is involved, right? So it makes sense to pray about your job search. To hand it over to Him to guide you to the right places, the right people. I mean, you could get a job on your own, and then have it be the absolute wrong fit. Ungodly people, negative energy. But if you turn your search over to God, and tune in to Him and His direction in your life, then you know that you're going to end up where He wants you to go."

Jasmine stared at him, mouth dropped. This guy was amazing. To look at him — tall, slim, exotic, gorgeous face — you would expect him to be self-centered and aloof. You would expect him to have had an easy life, everything handed to him. But he was anything but. His reality was entirely different. He claimed to be a "fledgling Christian," just learning the faith, but when he came out with stuff like that, it almost put her to shame. She'd followed Jesus her entire life. Why hadn't she thought of asking God to guide and bless her job search?

"I love that idea. In fact, want to say a quick prayer together?"

He nodded and closed his eyes. She began, "Dear Father, thank You for bringing Dax here to help me with my job search. Please guide me as I look for my first career stop. Lead me to the right people and the right place where You want me to be. Let's do this together, God. Amen."

She looked at him and smiled and he was beaming as well. "That's a good start. I'd repeat it along the way too."

"Okay." They dropped hands and she showed him the three outfits he'd be modeling for her. Then they started the fittings. She had a little bit of tailoring to do to make them fit him properly. She marked the alterations and set the clothes aside.

"How about some lunch? You must be starving."

He shrugged and then an undeniable rumbling sound came from his stomach. They laughed. "I was about to say I was fine, but my stomach has its own plans."

"Let's take my car, and I'll take you to a lunch place downtown Pittsburgh with great sandwiches and salads, then I can give you a little walking tour of the city."

"Sounds good."

They headed off. His legs were so long she knew he was scrunched in her little compact car. "Feel free to move the seat back if you're, you know, uncomfortable." He shook his head and waved off her concern, but she smiled a few minutes later when he started searching with his hand for the adjustment knob.

She pulled up in front of a favorite deli restaurant, Eat Unique, then drove past it and down a block to the right until she found a parking spot on the street. They left the car and walked back. They stood at the counter, gazing at the huge lit menu on the wall, then ordered and found a table.

"So tell me a little more about Pedro. And do you have any other boys you're mentoring?"

Dax had launched into a story about his young mentee when a waitress brought their selections: Jasmine the white turkey chili and greens salad, and Dax the pesto chicken sandwich. Both lunches hit the spot, and when they pushed their plates away, they sat back and talked some more.

"I want to hear more about your sewing skills. Did they teach you that in college?"

"I've been sewing since I was a little girl. It was an activity I was drawn to, and my mom signed me up for lessons at the local Singer Sewing Machine store. Every Saturday I'd bound out of bed and my mom would take me to the store, and I'd have a three-hour group lesson. They had a classroom in the back with different models of sewing machines, so we got to try them all out. You got to pick your own pattern and make clothes at your own pace. It was heavenly."

He laughed and didn't say anything.

"I know. I was a total nerd. But this was something I loved! I don't know why."

"What were the other girls in your class like?"

"Twice as old as me. I was like nine, ten, and they were all in high school. I was there because I loved it, and they were there because they had Home Ec in school and needed remedial help. So after using the store-bought patterns a few projects in a row, I tried my hand at designing my own patterns. I designed a dress to fit myself, and made it, and I was hooked. I not only wore that poor thing every chance I got, but I told my parents I wanted my own sewing machine so I could sew more than once a week."

"What'd they say?"

"They let me pick out a sewing machine for Christmas."

He smiled at her and looked into her eyes. "They sound like awesome parents."

"They were. I had a great childhood." Then she frowned and rolled her eyes. Way to rub his nose in it. "Sorry, I didn't mean to …"

"What? You don't have to apologize for having great parents. Do you think I'd want you to have no parents and spend your childhood in the foster system, just because that's what I had?"

She thought about that, concentrating on his words. "No, I guess not. But it seems, I don't know, braggy to talk about my parents to you, how they took me to lessons to develop my interests, they bought me an expensive gift for Christmas. Especially when you had no one to do that stuff."

He reached over the table and placed his hands on hers. "I'm happy for you. I love to hear about happy childhoods, you know? It seems like those TV shows I used to watch.

Happy Days and *Wonder Years*. Did some kids grow up that way? Yes, sometimes they did. Life wasn't like that for me, but guess what? I grew up anyway, and now I'm an adult, and I'm doing my best to form my own life. And I learned a lot about what I wanted my life to be like, from what I didn't have as a child."

"You're making your dreams come true," she whispered, taken by him and his message.

"Well, I don't know if I'd go that far. But I know how much I benefitted from adults who helped me. Who were kind to me when they didn't have to be. When they changed their plans because I needed a little help. I paid attention to those things when I was a kid, and I've never forgotten those acts of kindness. So now, I'm an adult. It's my turn to pay that forward. So, I help others as often as I can. God was watching out for me as a kid in the system. I didn't realize that then, I didn't even know who He was. But I know it now. He used kind people, Christian people, to be His servants on earth. It made a difference to kids like me. And now, I do that as much as I can."

"You're amazing."

He pulled his hands into his lap. "No, I'm not. You're amazing. You have all this talent and spark and beauty."

She stared at him, then she leaned forward across the table and he met her halfway. They joined lips, just a happy, friendly brush. "I'm glad we met."

"Me too."

They settled the bill and walked outside. They strolled to the cross street where the car was parked, but instead of turning right, Jasmine looked left. "Hey! I just thought of something. Let's go this way."

They walked several blocks. Jasmine pulled out her phone and went to the Notes section where she'd typed in an address a week ago. They were close. Very close. She would start the photo shoot tomorrow, and she still had alterations and pressing to do when they got home, so they might as well have some fun today.

"Are you up for a walk?"

"Sure, I've been sitting all day."

They went to Fifth Avenue, and they turned and set a pretty fast pace. It felt good to stretch their legs. Jasmine pointed out places of interest. About twenty minutes later, they were on the corner of Fifth and Penn. "Okay, this is it," she said uncertainly. Of course, there were four corners on the corner of Fifth and Penn. Which was the right one?

Dax was looking around for a milestone. "This is what?"

Jasmine scanned the corner. Phone booths weren't nearly as prevalent now as they were close to fifty years ago. Did phone booths even exist anymore in the age when everyone had a personal cell phone? Then she squealed. "Over here!" She grabbed Dax's hand and, seeing the Walk indicator, dashed across the street. They waited for the light to change, then they crossed the block again, and there, on the corner, was a phone booth.

She was quite sure it wasn't the same exact booth that her mother had been left in. The newspaper article had described it, and it was a full booth, one a person would walk into, close the door behind them and be totally isolated from the street. This one was more modern. It had a plastic shell but only encircled the caller from the waist up, and there was no door. A shelf and a phone, and a plastic overhang to cover your head.

This street corner was part of her family history.

"What's going on?" Dax asked and Jasmine pulled herself back from her thoughts. Her heart raced with her discovery.

"This phone booth," she said and ran a hand over it, "has meaning in my family."

He looked confused.

"I was looking for a camera in my dad's spare room closet. And I ran into a folder full of old documents — newspaper articles and few other papers. I got curious and read them all, and I uncovered a family secret I'd never been told before."

He watched her carefully, and at her words, his eyebrows went up. "About this phone booth?"

She laughed. "I know it sounds crazy, but yes! Listen. My mom was born, and then two days later, she was abandoned in this phone booth. Or, well, a phone booth on this street corner. I assume the original booth was eventually replaced by this one. Someone, I'm assuming her mother, delivered her in a basket to the phone booth on this corner. She was discovered by a man named Paul Mason, and he took her to the hospital. She was examined, fed, hydrated, and kept a few days but she was fine. The hospital put her up for adoption, and just days later, she was adopted by my grandparents, Ken and Adele Somers."

He nodded. "Babies are almost always adopted." He looked up at her. "I mean, easier than older kids."

"So, they signed the papers, took her home and raised her. They told her about her story, but she never cared about pursuing it. I mean, I never heard this story at all until I stumbled onto those old clippings. But for a few weeks, my mom, as a baby, was all over the Pittsburgh news! The Phone Booth Baby."

He laughed. "Great story. Great ending, it sounds like."

"But that's just it. We don't know the ending."

"Sure we do. Your mom got adopted by her forever parents and lived happily ever after."

"But what about the rest of it? Who left her in that phone booth? Why did they do it? Was it her mother? What happened to her parents? What was their story?"

Dax shrugged. "Does it matter?"

"Does it matter? Of course it does! I might have grandparents out there I never knew I had."

"But you do have grandparents, right? Your mom's parents? And, for that matter, your dad's?"

"Well, yes, but I could have more. I don't know. I'm just curious. I feel like this is a mystery I want to solve. Need to solve. And we have so many resources at our disposal now that they never had back in the late sixties. We have the internet, social media. Hey," she took a step into the phone booth, "maybe I can put a poster up here in the phone booth. Maybe someone remembers the incident, knows something. Just think about the poor young mom who gave her up. Maybe she comes here to remember her. If I had a poster up here with contact information, maybe we could connect."

Dax let out a breath. "Jasmine, you said your mother doesn't care, right?"

"Right."

"So," he stopped and shrugged, "why do you?"

"It's tugged my interest. I don't have a better reason than that. I just want to see if I can figure anything out."

"Your mom found her real parents, and they did a great job raising her, I assume. They are loving parents and now grandparents. Why dig up a past that everyone wants to keep buried? Do you think you might hurt their feelings with this?"

Jasmine considered. "I hadn't thought of it that way."

Dax reached out and patted the plastic shell of the phone booth. "My advice? Leave it alone."

Jasmine looked back at the booth. She was busy right now with the job search. She'd think about this more later.

Chapter Nine

That evening, around seven, her dad came home from work. Jasmine was accustomed to him arriving home late, sometimes exhausted and drawn. Orthopedic surgeons didn't always pull nine-to-five hours. Plus, he was careful about inserting exercise into his schedule, so sometimes he was arriving home after a sweaty workout. She and Dax had assembled homemade pizzas and planned to put them in the oven to bake when Dad arrived home. It was important to Dax to get to know him a little better, so it was important to Jasmine too.

What Jasmine wasn't accustomed to was the dynamic of her father around a guy she was interested in. She'd been away at college for the last four years, and back in high school, Mom was always around to make her boyfriends feel welcome and loved. But of course, things had changed.

"He's not real warm and fuzzy," she'd warned Dax several times this evening as they loaded a couple pre-formed pizza crusts with cheese, sauce, pepperoni and vegetables. "He's a great guy, but I guess you just have to get to know him."

"That's what tonight's for," he assured her. She was still nervous, despite his casual "I can handle anything you throw at me" grin.

Of course, her dad knew Dax had arrived today. He knew Dax was staying a few days to help out with her photos. And although they hadn't gone into an in-depth discussion about her and Dax's relationship, she'd dropped enough hints for her dad to realize that this guy may be a special one. *And don't you dare do anything to mess that up. Or embarrass me.* She didn't say that outright, but she hoped that her mental telepathy was working well enough so that when she said, "We want to make him feel welcome, don't we, Daddy?" that he knew she really meant, "Don't chase him away. Please."

So, at seven o'clock, the door from the garage opened, and her dad walked into the kitchen, looking tired from a long day that had started probably thirteen hours before. He gave Jasmine a quick smile, then looked up at Dax. "Oh, hey."

"Hi. How was your day?"

Dad chuckled and took his time answering while he walked across the kitchen to rest his gym bag on one of the barstools facing the tall counter. "One knee replacement, a torn labrum repair, and a thumb tendon repair. That was all before noon. Rounds at the hospital before office appointments, then finish up with a workout at the gym." He went to the refrigerator and pulled out a fruit juice. "All in a day's work, I guess."

"Wow," Dax said, admiration on his face. "Think how many people you helped today. Think how many lives you touched, between the patients, their families and their friends. Amazing."

Her dad looked over at him, and studied the younger man. Jasmine knew why. He was looking for signs of insincerity or sarcasm. But he wasn't going to find it here. He may not know Dax real well yet, but Dax was one of, no, *the* most sincere person she'd ever met. He truly admired her dad. He wouldn't have said all that if he hadn't. Dad must've come to the same conclusion. He took a gulp of his fruit juice, wiped his mouth and said, "Well, thank you, Dax. I guess you're right. It's easy to forget when you do it day after day."

Jasmine felt a wash of shame come over her. It was so easy to take her dad for granted. To take his life's work for granted. He'd been a surgeon for as long as she'd known him. Sure, she knew he worked hard. She knew he healed people. But she'd never given it much thought. It was just what he did. She'd never considered the toll it took on him — physical and emotional. She'd never even asked him about his profession. When was the last time she'd asked him how his day was, and what challenges he'd faced? She couldn't remember when, that's when. And yet Dax asked the minute Dad had walked in.

And wait, who was the one of them who was supposed to know about families?

Dax opened the oven door and slid the pizzas in. "Hope you don't mind me making myself at home in your kitchen. But sounds like you could use a good, home-cooked meal, as soon as possible. Jasmine and I fixed up these pizzas. They'll be ready in fifteen minutes."

Dad smiled at him, then her. He hadn't expected them to cook for him. Jasmine hoped upon hope that he hadn't grabbed something on the way home.

"That's very thoughtful of you, thank you. I'll run up, take a quick shower and change, and be back, ready to eat."

As he walked by Jasmine, he leaned to give her a peck on the cheek. She laid a palm on his face, an affectionate gesture she couldn't remember ever using with her dad. He breezed by her with a smile and left the room. She looked over at Dax. He was setting the timer so the pizzas wouldn't burn. She closed her eyes and prayed silently, *Lord, thank You for leading Dax into my life. Into our lives. Let me be more like him. Let me find the good in people, and let me think less about myself.*

She finished her thought and opened her eyes. He was focused on her, and smiled. She felt her cheeks heat, and knew she was probably blushing. Might as well come clean, she thought. "I was saying a prayer of thanks for you."

Now it was his turn to blush. "Really? Because of my pizza-making skills?"

She laughed. "No. You're very … special. I hope you know that."

He frowned and shook his head. "Special? I'm not sure if that's a good thing."

She crossed the room and went up on her tiptoes, laid a kiss on his lips. "Believe me, it's a very good thing." She pulled away. "Thanks for being here."

His smile was enough to make her heart trip. This guy had a killer smile. Combined with the face, hair, eyes — *man!* But it was his heart that completed the package.

Dad returned, the scent of Irish Spring accompanying him, his hair still damp at his neck. Jasmine realized he was calm and comfortable in the company of her and Dax. It was Dax who'd done that. They sliced the pizzas, formed a smorgasbord, and filled their plates, then ate on the couch in front of the TV tuned to a baseball game.

Later, after she'd walked Dax upstairs, made sure he had everything he needed, and said good night, she went to her own room and closed the door. She quickly went through her nighttime routine and settled into bed. They were getting an early start for the photo shoot in the morning and she wanted to be rested. She heard her dad's footsteps pause outside her door, then a faint tapping before he opened it and stepped inside. The light from the hallway illuminated her room enough for him to casually take in the scene.

"You all settled?" he said with a hint of distraction. His head turned, looking into every corner of her room.

"Daddy, what are you looking for?" she asked, as if she didn't know.

"Nothing."

"You're looking for Dax, aren't you? He's not in here."

He knew he'd been nabbed. He rolled his eyes and laughed.

"You like him, Dad?"

"Sure."

"Seriously, when was the last time I ever brought a date home and we spent an entire evening with you?"

He pretended to think. "Never."

"But it was fun."

"Quite pleasant."

"He's an unusual guy. I could learn a lot from him."

Tim shrugged and backed out of the room. He blew her a kiss. She fell asleep with a smile.

* * *

The next day, she packed the clothes into the car, hanging on hangers inside garment bags. She'd made the alterations and steam-pressed the garments to within an inch of their lives. They needed to look their absolute best for the photos, so she forbade Dax from putting any of them on, just to go sit in her car and cause creasing. So he'd have to change into the clothes at the photo site.

Which was outside. She couldn't think of a great indoor venue where she could photo him without distractions, but

Pittsburgh offered a ton of outdoor options. Maybe he could slip into a public bathroom to change.

He came down to the kitchen. She loved a guy who was prompt. Fresh from the shower, he not only smelled awesome, but he looked even better. His complexion was flawless, his eyes warm and happy, and his hair — he could charge to give advice to hairdressers who wanted to offer his look to their clients. It always looked perfect and effortless.

"Are you ready? You look great."

"I'm ready. Mind if I grab something to eat first, though?" He brushed a casual two fingers over her hand and she almost lost her ability to breathe.

"Of course. In fact, I went out early and got these." She pulled out a box with half a dozen donuts. "I didn't know what kind you liked, or even if you liked donuts at all, so I got a variety. Oh, and these too." She lifted two cups of strong coffee from the donut shop.

Perusing her selections, she internally kicked herself. Donuts? On the morning of a photo shoot? Maybe, as slim as he was, he actually watched his weight. Or, hello! He worked in the healthcare field — maybe he didn't approve of fatty foods. She rushed on before he could respond, "You know what? I changed my mind." She picked up the box of donuts and began to put them away, saying, "How about some eggs? I could make you something healthy …."

He took a step closer and scooped the box out of her hands. "Don't you dare commandeer the donuts."

"You like them?" she asked cautiously.

"Of course I do! Who doesn't like donuts?" He surveyed the choices and pulled out a chocolate-frosted one, taking a big bite. Then his eyes drifted shut and he moaned with pleasure. "So good. Which one do you want?"

She grabbed a jelly-filled and handed him his coffee, secretly pleased. She was a donut girl from way back.

They got into Jasmine's car and drove to Emerald View Park. Her compact car had a little trouble getting up the side of Mt. Washington, chugging its loud resistance to the plan. Jasmine explained, "Pittsburgh is a city that values its greenery. We have six parks within the city limits, and that doesn't even count the rivers. Emerald sits at the very top of Mt. Washington. It's a little hard to get to, with as little an engine as this car has, but it's so worth it. There's a spot I love going to, called Overlook Point. It has a statue of George Washington and his Indian guide. There's a little brick platform and wall, and it overlooks the entire skyline of the city."

Dax was nodding his head, then turned and looked at her. "George Washington had an Indian guide?"

"Yeah, who knew? Pretty amazing. We had to learn his guide's name in school, and what part of history he played, but I can't remember it now. Anyway, it'll be a great spot to do the photo shoot. There will be all kinds of backdrops depending on where you stand."

They finally made it and Jasmine parked the car. Dax grabbed the garment bags from the back and they walked to Overlook Point. The city looked beautiful, clean and sparkling, as if it knew it had an important role today, and was anxious to please.

"Nice choice," Dax murmured, looking out over the high rises in the distance, some black, some silver, a solitary red, and several earth-tone browns.

"Thanks. Now, I'm calling the outfits one, two and three, one being the most casual and three the most dressy — the suit, obviously. I'm going to start with one, then move up the dressy scale. So, could you go find a place you're comfortable to change, and get suited up in one?"

Dax pulled his attention away from her and glanced around. Not a single building occupied Overlook Point. Not only that, no other tourists were there either. Not a person in sight. Dax looked back at her and shrugged. "I'm game if you are." In a single, graceful swipe, he pulled his tee shirt over his head. He dropped it carelessly onto the ground beside him. Next, he unbuttoned his cargo shorts and let them drop. Before she knew it, he stood before her in nothing but his boxer briefs.

Jasmine gulped and felt her eyes go wide. No, no, no. She was a professional. Or, she wanted to be soon. Models got dressed and undressed in the weirdest places all the time. It was just part of the gig. They didn't think twice about it. Even though said models sported strong, sturdy legs and amazingly tight abs. Stop staring, and … *stop staring!*

She shrugged, forced her best attempt at nonchalance and giggled. "Sure, why not?" She turned her back and dragged herself to study the light and her camera and make decisions about where to shoot him. All the while, she took deep breaths to slow her racing heart. Fortunately, when she turned back to him, he was fully clothed.

Then it was down to business. She placed him where she wanted him, then gave him instructions, "Left foot up on the brick wall. Left hand on your leg. Look away for a profile. Now look at me, right into the lens. Smile. Now serious."

She was amazed how natural he looked in her viewfinder, as if he'd modeled before. But he'd told her he hadn't. Reviewing the digital shots, she realized he had a lock of hair hanging down in front of his eyes. She stepped over to him and brushed it away, her fingers trailing his forehead, then his cheek. He smiled at the contact and they met gazes. Before she could give thought to her impulse, she kissed him. A long, intentional joining of their lips that put a dash of color in his cheeks, and she was sure, hers too. She pulled away with a smile and went back to work.

"Time for two. I think I've got all I need with one."

He joined her at the spot where they'd stacked the other garment bags. She handed him his next change of clothes. He took it from her, then looked at her, eyebrows up. "I embarrassed you before, didn't I?"

"No!" she insisted, although, of course he had. "Not at all."

"I can go looking around for a private place if you want."

She took a deep breath and let it out. "Don't be silly. I'll just turn my back. No problem."

Behind her, she heard him taking one outfit off and putting the next on. "Ready."

And he was. He looked great in two, and they launched into their routine, their dance that they were quickly perfecting. Before she knew it, she had enough of two and moved to three.

Dax looked shiny and perfect in the suit, and she couldn't help telling him so. He seemed pleased. "I've never owned one."

"Really? You should. With your body, you were made to wear a suit."

"A suit is an expense I can't afford right now, and honestly, I have nowhere to wear it. I wear scrubs to work. I wear jeans and shorts and tee shirts. My idea of dressing up is having buttons on my shirt."

Her smile lingered, then she took in the beauty of her Dax in a dressy suit.

Her Dax.

When had she started thinking of him in that way?

She proceeded with many of the same poses and backgrounds that she'd liked before, this time with three. When she finally decided she was done, she had nearly three hundred photos, and that was after immediately deleting ones that were blurry or uncentered. Three hundred good ones — how would she ever decide which ones to print for her portfolio?

"We're done," she announced and he whooped. He'd been a great sport. He hadn't complained at all after ... how long? She pulled out her cell and looked. "Oh, my gosh, Dax, you should have told me. We've been at this for five hours! You must be exhausted. You poor thing!"

"No, it was fun."

"I've barely given you breaks! Your feet must hurt from standing all day."

He shook his head. "I stand all day at work, remember? I'm fine. I was happy to help."

She grabbed both his arms as she faced him. "I owe you a huge thank you. How about dinner out tonight, just the two of us? My treat."

His agreement came without hesitation.

* * *

Dax stared into the bathroom mirror in Jasmine's dad's house. He wanted to look good for her, for their dinner date. He rubbed a hand over his chin, then through his hair. He shrugged. Yeah, he looked okay.

He turned away, then back again. Staring closer into the mirror, he wondered if he could take a step back and view himself as Jasmine saw him. Forget the fact that his face was familiar to him. What did she see when she looked at him? What did she see in him? Had she looked beyond the surface?

His whole life, he'd never had trouble attracting women. He supposed he was a good-enough-looking guy, always had been. His looks were never the problem. It was his sense of self-worth that he'd always needed to work on.

Years of therapy provided by the state taught him that just because his parents had given him up, had passed him around, then finally given up on him and offered him up for adoption, didn't mean he wasn't worthy of being loved, or having a family care for him. And, as the years of foster care stretched on without a family wanting to adopt him, same message: he was worthy of love, it just wasn't happening. Then, his eighteenth birthday arrived and he was no longer eligible for adoption. He was an adult. On his own. Independent, and he needed to make his own way in the world.

He'd experienced some good foster parents over the years. Some good counselors. Some coaches and adults who reached out and made a difference for him. He considered those his parental figures – just in dribs and drabs. But he'd reached out and grabbed those jewels of wisdom and internalized them. When most kids – either with or without parents – didn't pay attention, or even rolled their eyes when adults gave advice, Dax listened. He considered. It was probably the best he was going to get and he wasn't going to pass it up.

He'd become a responsible adult, that was his goal. He'd never succumbed to problems with drugs, alcohol, breaking the law, like so many kids without parents did. He controlled that himself. He was a good person, fundamentally.

But still, that voice in the back of his head always made an appearance whenever he started a new relationship: *why do you think she likes you? What makes you think she'll stick around? What will happen when she figures out you're unlovable?*

So, he generally held back, played it cool, didn't get too invested. It seemed to be the personality women expected, to go along with his looks. As a result, he'd never fallen in love, not really. He'd had crushes. He'd felt attractions to certain women. But falling in love required a person to open up and talk, and not only get to know the other person, but to allow them to get to know you. To become vulnerable to pain in case you lay your heart out there, and the woman stomps on it, not interested in returning that love. And that's where he had absolutely no experience at all. No track record to call on. No love in his life.

Then came Jasmine, who was suddenly changing all that. Something about Jasmine made him want to talk to her, to reveal his secrets, to expose his past, his present realities, and his dreams for the future. He wanted to spend hours talking to her – finding out those funny stories from her childhood, what she was like during college, her plans for building her future. She came from a loving family, despite the fact that her parents recently divorced. She'd felt love and support as a child – took it for granted, surely. And she had known Christ her entire life. How different would he be, would his life be, if he'd been introduced to Jesus as a child? Would his childhood have changed at all? He wasn't sure but he had to assume it would.

But despite his best efforts, the fear that he could never quite push past, had taken root in this new relationship as well. He had no business being with a woman like Jasmine. The girl had grown up with a silver spoon in her mouth. She had no exposure to neglect. She had never wanted for anything, she was the princess of her parents' hearts. Her father, a surgeon, had made sure of that. What could he possibly give to a woman like her? Her life had been easy. His had been hard. She had everything she ever needed. He'd scraped by with the bare minimum.

And yet, with the abundance of love and family and acceptance in her life, she was going after more. He thought back to their conversation about the phone booth yesterday. At the risk of hurting her mother and grandparents, she was interested in searching out this possibility of another grandmother. She was focused on solving this hidden family mystery, despite her mother not wanting her to. Asking her not to.

When was enough, enough? Was Jasmine so accustomed to getting whatever she wanted in life, that she didn't know when to quit? And if so, how could *he* possibly ever make her happy? He wasn't equipped. And that mindset was so foreign to his own.

He shook his head and turned away from the mirror. He swiped his hands down his clothes, brushing out any wrinkles that could be there.

He was walking unmapped territory here. He didn't have a clear idea how Jasmine felt about him, whether she was interested in a relationship of some kind. Did he want to pursue her, despite their obvious differences in backgrounds and lifestyles, and the long distance between them? Would he be walking into a future of disaster if he pursued it?

He pursed his lips in concentration and walked to the door. Was she the right one for him? Or were there just too many differences and warning signs to ignore? He wished he had a dad, or even an older brother to help him through this. But of course, he didn't. Instead, he bowed his head and said a fervent prayer for help and guidance so he handled this tricky situation gracefully.

He went downstairs and took a seat on the living room couch. Moments later, Jasmine walked in, wearing a simple, navy blue dress that skimmed her knee and showed off her trim, fit arms with a sleeveless style. She'd put some time into her makeup and hair. His mouth dropped open and he came to his feet almost reverently.

"You look beautiful."

She beamed a smile at him and giggled like she didn't know that any male of any age would think the same thing upon the sight of her.

"Seriously, you look gorgeous." He leaned in and kissed her softly, careful not to mess her lipstick, a shiny pink that he wondered briefly if he now had on his own lips, too.

"Thank you."

The sound of her pleased voice did something to him and his pulse started racing, like he had high-octane caffeine racing through his veins.

"I say the same back to you: you look gorgeous too, Dax." She reached up and brushed her fingers through his hair. She seemed to like touching it, and of course, he liked her touching it, too. He enjoyed her touch wherever it happened to land on him and he hoped she never stopped. "Well. You must be starving. Let's go," she said.

"Okay, but ..." she turned and looked at him, "you've been driving me around your town all weekend. Tonight, I drive, and you ride."

"Sounds good. I'll navigate."

She directed him to the restaurant, and he found parking on the street. They strolled past the river and came to the door of LeMont restaurant. The hostess was expecting them, and led them to a table by the window overlooking a view of the city. The buildings, after dark, were practically sparkling. She could not have picked a more romantic location for the two of them to share dinner.

The hostess left them to review the menus, and he spotted the prices. He gasped so hard that it turned into a cough, then, unable to get control of himself, he started choking. Jasmine's head flew up from her menu and her eyes popped wide in alarm. She jumped to her feet and came behind him, pounding him on the back. He tried to dissuade her, don't trouble yourself, he'd get it under control in a minute. But he couldn't get the words out. Other diners were beginning to stare.

She lifted his water glass and coaxed him to take small sips between coughs. She continued patting his back, and coached him, "Breathe. Breathe. Breathe."

Eventually, his coughing spell passed. Of course, he probably looked like he'd been through a battle. "I'm sorry," he said, and rose. "Let me just use the men's room. I'll be right back."

She still looked worried. "Are you all right?"

"I'm fine. I'll be right back."

He practically sprinted to the facilities and turned on the water, letting it run over his hands, then he raised it to his face and splashed cold water several times. His breathing was coming more normal now.

Dang it! He was a fish out of water in a fancy restaurant like this. He didn't belong here and he wasn't fooling anyone. But Jasmine was at home in the posh surroundings. She'd practically grown up in places like this. How would a guy like him ever impress and interest a sophisticated woman like Jasmine? Who did he think he was? Jasmine deserved much better than an orphan adult, all alone in the world. She had it on the ball.

As much as he didn't want it to be true, they were mismatched. Unless he put the brakes on now, he'd be charging head-on into a boat-load of heartache. For himself and for her. They would never make it as a couple.

Anxiety gripped him. He'd come to this realization, now, how should he handle it? Should he go out there and break up with Jasmine right now? Explain what was most likely already obvious to her — that they were doomed before they even got started? But then, he'd have to drive back to New York late tonight. Maybe instead, he should just tell her in the morning. Or, he could enjoy spending the whole weekend with her, and call her with his break-up decision next week. But that seemed uncourageous.

Uncertain, he glanced back at the mirror. His complexion color had returned to about normal. He grabbed a tissue and blew his nose, then shook his hair back from his face. He stood quietly for a moment and let his breathing slow.

That's when it occurred to him. It was the small voice speaking to him again, the voice of a young abandoned boy whose family didn't want him, the voice of the young man who'd grown up in hundreds of different families, but none of them he could call his own. That was the destructive voice he'd come to recognize as a child that was lying to him.

He knew how to deal with that voice now. He may not have a father, but he had a Father – a heavenly one who was always in his corner. Always had his back, always wanted to help. So he closed his eyes and prayed, *God, help me with this.*

Did You introduce Jasmine to me for a reason? Is there a divine plan here? If so, help me not to screw it up. Help me step by step.

He waited. The Bible talked about a peace that passes all understanding. Dax knew what it felt like, because he'd experienced it before, often right after a prayer. That's what he needed right now — a peace to settle over him so he could pull himself together and handle this crisis like God wanted him to, not like his fear was urging him to.

He needed an answer guide. Did God want him and Jasmine to be together? What about his fears about her life of opportunity and wealth, so different from his? Would that destroy them? Or, in their differences, could they help each other? He could help her see his view of the world, and she could share hers with him?

As he walked back to the table, he coached himself silently, *Take it easy. God's with you. You're fine.* When he slid back into his chair he forced a smile and said, "Sorry about that. Didn't mean to alarm you."

Jasmine said with a sigh of relief, "Oh thank goodness! You had me worried there."

"Now, can we talk about these prices?" He pointed at the menu.

"No. I said my treat, and I meant it."

"Jasmine, no. You could've taken me for a hamburger and I would've been completely happy."

"But if I took you for a hamburger, you would've missed the best view in the city." She lifted a hand and gestured, Vanna White-style.

He studied her face. "But you don't have a job ..."

"No. But my dad does." She reached into her purse and whipped out a credit card. "My dad insisted. I called him this afternoon and told him all about the photo shoot, and how great you did with the poses, and how awesome my portfolio is going to be. He was so happy, he offered to pay for our meal tonight."

His eyebrows went up with surprise. "Did you tell him you picked the most expensive place in the city?"

"In fact, he suggested it."

"He did?"

"Yes. So, quit worrying, quit choking, and pick out your meal. Oh, and why don't we start with an appetizer?"

Chapter Ten

The following morning, Dax carried his bag out to his car and tossed it into the back seat. Jasmine trailed him, her heart like a big lump in her throat. He was going home. He had a job to return to in New York, and she had a job search to continue in Pennsylvania.

He turned and slipped his arms around her, pulling her in easily for an embrace. She tucked her face into his solid chest and squeezed him while she inhaled his scent. She had to remember it. Who knew when she'd see him again?

If ever?

That thought made her pulse trip, making her feel a little panicky. Of course she'd see him again. But when? And why? What reason did she have to entice him for another visit? He'd offered to help her with her photo shoot, and now that was done.

They parted and he said, "Thank you for your hospitality. It was nice."

"Thank *you* for your modeling skills. Those photos are great and they'll give me the start of a good portfolio for these employers."

They stood quietly, staring into each other's eyes, hesitant to say good-bye. *Say something.* If she let him drive off without a plan for a next get-together, she'd never forgive herself.

"So, let me ask," she started, but she'd interrupted him. He'd spoken at the same time. "Go ahead."

"No, you."

She shook her head and laughed. "You."

"Okay. I'm going to just put this out there. If you say yes, it'll be a good drive home. If you say no, I can sneak off and lick my wounds."

She smiled. "Yes."

He laughed. "Yes what?"

"I don't know, but of the two choices, yes sounds much better."

He reached for her hands and squeezed them. "I'd like to see you again. In fact, I'd like to see where this ... thing ... might go. This relationship. I like you, Jasmine."

"I like you, too." She sounded like a little girl, professing her love and commitment to a boy on the playground. But he didn't seem to mind because his face was beaming with happiness.

"Great."

"Are you talking about a long-distance relationship? Like, boyfriend and girlfriend?"

"Yes. We see each other whenever we can. And we call, text or IM whenever possible." He pulled her closer. "I know you deserve better. You deserve someone close by who can take you out every night and spoil you. And believe me, I have no idea if it's going to work. But I have to wonder if God put us together for a reason. It'll be hard being apart, but I'd like to give it a try. If you do."

"I'd like that." She had a boyfriend. Wow. When was the last time she could say that?

He pulled her closer and leaned his forehead against hers. He said in a whisper, "We are so different, Jasmine."

She nodded. "I know we are. But just our pasts. I think who we are now, we're more alike than you think."

He pulled back and looked into her eyes. "What do you mean?"

She shrugged. "So, our childhoods were very different, obviously. But what are our priorities now? Mine are starting my career, working hard and making it on my own. Same as yours, right?"

He nodded.

"I know a priority of yours is to learn more about God and live a Christian life. Same as me. The fact that I've been doing it awhile longer doesn't mean that I have all the answers. I can learn so much from you. It's important to me that we have similar faiths."

He grinned. "When you put it that way, it makes me think maybe our differences aren't that big."

The way he said it, gave her a little jolt. "Are you concerned about our differences? I mean, are you worried about them?"

He quieted, then squeezed her hands. "I want to be honest with you. Yes, I am worried. You're used to getting everything you want in life. If we end up together, there's no way I could provide that to you."

She swatted his shoulder. "You make me sound like a spoiled brat."

He shook his head but stayed somber. "I don't mean it like that, exactly. It's just that you look at life differently than I do. You have no boundaries. Anything is possible to you, nothing is off limits."

She thought about that. "I'm not sure that's entirely true. But even if it were, that doesn't mean that I'd expect you to give it to me. Believe me, I've learned a lot already about growing up and being an adult. If I want anything in life, I have to work hard for it. It's not going to be handed to me."

"Okay," he said, drawn out like he didn't quite believe it.

"I know my entire life hasn't been hard like yours, but the last year hasn't exactly been a picnic. And now that I'm trying to make my own way in the world, I want to be self-supporting. And the way to do that is to do your best and work hard."

"And be grateful for the blessings that you have, and know when to stop wanting more."

She cocked her head. She wasn't sure what point he was making there, but she had to agree the statement was sound. "Yep."

He pulled her into a hug and she savored his scent by breathing him deep into her lungs.

"So," she said playfully, "if we're going to go the official boyfriend/girlfriend route, then I say we need an official couple selfie."

He laughed and she pulled her cell phone out of her pocket. They both leaned against his car and she held her phone high in the air and snapped it. Then they kissed and she snapped it again.

"It's a start," she said with a laugh.

"Now, what was it you were going to say before?" he asked.

She stared at him. Oh yeah, she'd totally forgotten. She was going to see if she could interest him in visiting her again. "Not a thing."

"You don't remember?"

She leaned in close to him. "We already covered it."

That got her another kiss and a soft caress of his hand on her check. Then, he got in the car, started it, rolled down his window.

"Drive safe, boyfriend." She stood back and watched till he pulled out of sight.

* * *

It took two solid days to pore over the hundreds of shots she'd taken of Dax. It was nearly impossible to pick out the best ones. Probably because it was difficult to eliminate any. They were all good. The man was impossibly photogenic. She'd find herself staring at him, her heart about to burst because of the excitement caused by their relationship status. He was *hers*. Just the thought of it made her blood rush more forcefully.

She'd have to jolt herself back to work.

She eventually ended up with a sizable but manageable group of photos for the male side of her portfolio. Next she'd have to work on her female selections. And possibly, her children's fashions.

But first, she'd take a break. She pulled her computer onto her lap and accessed Facebook. She loaded in the two selfies of her and Dax and changed her relationship status to "In a Relationship." She paused, then checked her Newsfeed. Within seconds, her computer went crazy beeping as non-stop notifications hit her account. She laughed and spent the next hour responding to her friends that yes, she was in a relationship, his name was Dax, he lived in New York, she was currently in Pittsburgh, and yes oh yes, he sure was handsome!

She went back to her room and set her laptop on her desk. The manila folder of Phone Booth Baby clippings was sitting there and it fell to the floor. Jasmine picked it up and stared at it. Both her mother and Dax had advised her against pursuing this family mystery any further. Her mother, because she was happy with how her childhood had turned out, and had no interest in pursuing her true identity. Dax, since he had no relatives at all, couldn't understand why someone with an abundance of family members would need to track down more.

She should leave well enough alone. She didn't have time for this, and no one thought it was a good idea anyway. But if that was all true, why couldn't she put it behind her?

This was a mystery aching to be solved. Nothing interesting or unique had ever happened to her family. This was unique. Her mom was a celebrity of sorts, if only for a few days when she was an infant.

Her mom's birthday was coming up soon. Which meant that the anniversary of her being placed in the phone booth was coming up, too. She knew it was a long shot, and probably a very romantic notion, but what if her mom's mother made a special trip back to the phone booth every year on her baby's birthday, or the date she'd delivered her to the phone booth, to commemorate what must have been a very difficult decision she'd made as a young woman? God forbid, if Jasmine had ever had to make that horrible decision, she'd get sentimental about it every year. She'd never forget her daughter, and she'd never stop wondering what became of her.

Even if this mystery mother never made contact, it would give her comfort to know what her daughter had made of her life. Was she happy? Was she successful? And knowing that, would it make it worth the terrible decision she'd had to make way back when?

She thought for a few seconds more before she opened her laptop again. She opened up her word processing program, pondered her wording, and then typed,

"Do you remember the Pittsburgh Phone Booth Baby? On June 9, 1968 a baby girl was abandoned in this very phone booth. A passerby discovered her and delivered her to the hospital, where it was determined that she was healthy, and approximately 48 hours old. If you know any details that would help this family discover the identity of this baby's parents, please contact us. We appreciate your help."

She left her cell phone number but no name. She enlarged the size of the font to as big as she could fit on one page. She printed it out, grabbed a roll of tape from the kitchen drawer and jumped in her car.

* * *

That evening, Jasmine called her mother. She purposely omitted discussing the fact that she'd reopened the Phone Booth Baby case by taping her mini-poster inside the phone booth where her mom had been abandoned. It was a long shot anyway, considering Leslie was now in her late forties. Even if Leslie's birth mother had come back to the phone booth every year on the anniversary of Leslie's birth, or the date she'd abandoned her there, it probably would've only lasted a few years. A decade, at most. Not over forty-five years. But still, it was worth a try. She was leaving it in God's hands. If it was God's will for this mother to find her long-lost daughter, maybe God would use this poster as a way to make it happen.

But there were plenty of other things to talk about with her mom.

"So, I now have over twenty-five photos of Dax wearing my male fashions, three different outfits. We went to the top of Outlook Point on Mt. Washington."

"Oh, my. I can just picture the backdrop. The whole city."

"Yes, the setting was fantastic. I literally took hundreds of photos and it took me forever to whittle them down. I'm sure I probably eliminated some good ones but I'm happy with the ones I ended up with for my portfolio."

"Well, he's very photogenic."

"Mmmm."

"And very handsome."

Jasmine laughed. "You noticed that, did you?"

Her mom chuckled. "Yes, I did."

"I've got some other news, speaking of Dax."

Her mom's voice was smooth with a hint of humor as she said, "Oh really? What could that possibly be?"

"We're official. We're together. I mean, dating."

"I wondered! Congratulations, sweetheart. He seems like a very nice guy."

"He is. I mean, he amazes me each time I talk to him. He had the most horrible upbringing, but he's formed himself into a good man, despite all odds. He knows more about the Bible than I do, and he has better instincts about prayer and meditation, even though I've grown up as a Christian. I guess he knows what the other side of life is like, the non-Christian life, unlike me. And he likes this better, you know?"

"That's wonderful. I didn't know he had such a strong faith. All I could tell when we were in New York was that he cares for you, deeply. He took care of you during your injury and he sacrificed his job to make sure you were safe and taken care of. You can tell from how he looks at you that he cares about you. In my book, he's a keeper."

Jasmine sighed. "Yeah, the only thing is, of course, the distance. Why couldn't I have met him when I'd first gone to college instead of two days before I was leaving? Doesn't seem fair."

"God probably has His reasons."

"Have you ever had a long-distance relationship?"

"Not really."

"I mean, if we were long-term and committed, we'd be making plans together. But I'm doing my job search. I'll go anywhere for a good job in the fashion industry. What does that mean to him? I doubt if there's anything for me in Ithaca. Would I expect him to move for me if I got a job, say in New York City?"

"Whoa, way too early, honey. Take it a day at a time. Figure out if you like each other and get along before making plans to move him to another city."

Jasmine groaned. "It's so hard."

"Maybe one of God's lessons in this one is the old saying, let go and let God. We're not always in complete control of our lives. We need to be patient and let things unfold along with God's will."

"Hmmm. Patience is not one of my strong suits."

She laughed. "Yes, I've noticed."

They wandered back to the subject of the photo shoot. "So Mom, I have the men's fashions part of my portfolio covered now. But I don't want to be limited. I'm versatile. I want to show my women's fashions, and I even have some new ideas for children's designs."

"Okay, good. That would increase your employment opportunities."

"I can pull out the women's garments I designed and sewed for Senior Seminar. I think they're still good indications of my skill level. But I need someone to model them for me. Someone tall, slim, who moves well."

"I think I know just the candidate."

"Who?"

"Emma. Jeremy's wife."

Jasmine gasped. "Yes! She'd be perfect. She's so pretty and she fits the bill. With that mountain of hair, she'll be stunning in photos."

"Come on down to Pawleys and do the photo shoot on the beach! It'll be a great contrast to Dax's city shots."

"Wait. I'm having a brainstorm. If I take a few days, a week, to design and sew a couple children's outfits, I could have Stella model those. I could knock out both in the same trip."

"Great idea."

"I'll call Marianne to get Stella's measurements, and I'll call Emma for hers. We'll set something up in four, five days or so."

"Wow."

"Hey, I have to move on this to get those projects back to the employers who requested them. And, another benefit is we could celebrate your birthday while I'm there."

Leslie laughed. "True, that would be wonderful."

"Okay, it's all set, then. I'll get busy with alterations of Emma's garments, and designing and creating Stella's clothes. I'll keep you posted."

"Bye, honey."

* * *

The next four days were jam-packed with preparations for the remaining photo shoots. During a phone conversation, Emma graciously agreed to do the photo shoot and was looking forward to it. Armed with Emma's measurements, Jasmine altered the clothes she'd made for her Senior Seminar so they would fit her step-sister-in-law perfectly. Then she turned her focus to Stella's designs. Marianne was thrilled that Jasmine wanted to include her daughter in the project and she knew five-year-old Stella would be excited as well.

Jasmine pulled back from her table. What relation would Stella be to her? She had to do the math. Her mom had married Hank, so he was her stepfather. Hank had a daughter, Marianne and a son, Jeremy. They would be her step-siblings. Jeremy was married to Emma, who was her step-sister-in-law, and Marianne's daughter, Stella would be her step-niece.

Whew. Extended families got complicated. But all she had to do was drop the "step" on each of these people. She loved them all enough to consider them family, and they loved her too, and never failed to show it. That was all that mattered.

Dax called while she was drawing designs for Stella. "Hi … sweetie." He said it like he was trying it on for size, this new affection-based nicknaming, seeing how it would roll off the tongue.

She wasn't going to laugh at him outright, but it was funny, in a sweet sort of way. "Hi … darling."

He laughed. "Sorry."

"Don't be. I like it. Let's come up with sweet little nicknames we like. Um, baby?"

"Nah. Sweetheart?"

Jasmine shrugged. "It's okay. Loverboy?"

"Not sure."

"I don't know. I'm coming up empty here."

He made a tsking sound, then changed the subject. "What are you doing?"

"Working on designs for Stella. I've got a deadline now." She told him about her plan to travel to Pawleys Island, armed with the altered garments for Emma, and newly designed garments for Stella, and do their photoshoots on the beach. "So, I can get both of them in the same trip, and then my portfolio will be complete."

"For the stills. You still have to do the videos, right?"

Jasmine exhaled a bunch of air. "Oh, my gosh. I totally forgot about the videos. Dang it! Why didn't we do video of you when you were here?"

"I guess we both forgot about it."

"Well, good excuse to see each other again. Want to hit the road?"

"But you'll be going south."

"Oh, yeah."

"Here's an idea. Put all three of your models together in one video. We could do the video while we're at the beach."

An unbidden smile crept onto her face. "Did you say, we?"

"Sure."

"You'd come all the way to Pawleys Island to help me with the video?"

"Of course. I mean, I want to see you. I've never been to the beach. You need to make a video with me in it. Why not kill three birds with one stone?"

Her heart lightened so much, she felt giddy. "If you were here I'd kiss you so hard, you wouldn't know what hit you."

"Hold that thought. I'll look forward to it."

They quickly put together plans. Jasmine would kick butt on Stella's garments, Dax would drive to Pittsburgh, then together they'd drive to Pawleys, arriving in time for Leslie's birthday. When she hung up, she got to work. Nothing like a deadline to force productivity.

Chapter Eleven

The car was packed, all the garments in their bags hanging in the back seat. She was just waiting for Dax. Her excitement at seeing him again was intense. Maybe absence did make the heart grow fonder, but ever since they'd moved into a dating status, her thoughts were consumed by him. When she was busy working, or when she was relaxing, her mind turned to him. What was he doing? How was he feeling? Was he thinking about her? Did he miss her? She yearned for a more normal relationship where they could actually see each other without all this intense effort. But meanwhile, she was determined to enjoy it as it was.

Work on that patience thing that her mom had talked about.

To pass time, she flipped open her laptop and accessed her social media. On Twitter, she posted a tweet about her upcoming trip to the beach and reposted a photo of the ocean behind the Old Gray Barn that she'd first posted a few months ago when she was there for Jeremy and Emma's wedding.

On Facebook, she paged through her Newsfeed, seeing what her friends were up to. Another one of her classmates had found a job and was moving to California. She was happy for her, but urgently hoped that she'd have a job announcement to post, sooner rather than later.

As she paged through, she realized how much people were using Facebook now to spread messages for help to an extremely large audience. If a post went viral, it could reach hundreds of thousands, if not millions of people. Here was one about a lost child in Connecticut. Here was one from a teacher proving to her students how invasive the internet could be to their privacy, by how many hits the post would get. Here was one from a daughter: "If this post gets a million views, my father says he'll quit smoking."

Jasmine shook her head. She remembered fondly when Facebook consisted solely of her friends' news. Now it was like a community bulletin board with ads and requests for help. Only, the community was the whole world.

Then it dawned on her. What if she used Facebook and Twitter to help her with the Phone Booth Baby search? She'd gone to the trouble of posting a sign in the phone booth itself. How many people would that reach? Ten? Fifty? A hundred? Compared to the international reach of social media. What's the chance that her birth grandmother would see the post? Or at the very least, someone with information to share that would take her a step further in her stalled investigation.

She'd do it. What could it hurt? She wouldn't give her cell phone number. She'd just ask anyone with knowledge to comment on the post, or send her a private message. Maybe it would generate leads. She wouldn't have to follow up on them unless she wanted to.

Her mind made up, she pulled up the mini-poster she'd created, copied the wording and pasted it in a Facebook post. She made some minor revisions, added "Please Share" and released it to cyberspace. Then, she went to Twitter, and since it was restricted to so few characters, she tweeted a link to her Facebook post.

Done. If God wanted to lead someone to her, all she'd done was help Him along. God helps those who help themselves, wasn't that a Bible verse? She wasn't sure, but the philosophy was sound.

The doorbell rang and Jasmine screamed. She ran downstairs and there he was, on her doorstep. Her magnificent, heart-stopping boyfriend, here to pick her up for a couples' trip to the beach. She jumped up and fortunately he was ready for her — he held out his arms and caught her, and lowering his head, kissed his greeting.

"You look great," he murmured between breaths.

"You do, too."

Finally he placed her on her feet.

"I'm so glad you're here."

"Me too. My first trip to a beach …"

"Your first ever?" she interrupted. "That's a little hard to believe."

He considered that, his lip curling in concentration. "When have you been to the beach, I mean, before your mother moved there?"

"Every year! We'd take a family vacation and every summer we'd pick a different beach. All the way down the coast, we hit beach towns in Maryland, Delaware, Virginia, North and South Carolina, and down into Florida. Every summer of my entire childhood, we spent looking for the world's most perfect beaches. We …" Then she stopped, abruptly. How much of an idiot was she? "Oh Dax, I'm so sorry. I completely forgot that you didn't have that …"

"It's okay."

"No, it's not. I am so inconsiderate. Of course you didn't get to travel much as a kid. If at all. And since becoming an adult, you've been focused on school and work. I'm sorry."

He gave a grim smile and took her hands in his own. "Seriously, it's fine."

"Have you ever gone on vacation? Ever?"

He shrugged. "Sort of? I remember a couple group outings to an amusement park. About a dozen kids in the foster system got to go, and I was picked a few times. Man, it was fun. A bunch of ten- or eleven-year-olds racing around the park from one ride to another. The counselors knew they couldn't keep tabs on us so they just gave us hourly checkpoints. If we didn't show up, we'd have to sit in the bus for an hour, so of course we made sure we were there. Those were fun days. Once we stayed in a hotel. Swam in a pool, ate in the restaurant. That was fun." He grinned at her.

She reached up and put her hands on his cheeks. "Awww, you poor thing!"

But he took her hands and pulled them away. "No." His voice was firm, intense. She'd never heard that tone from him before. "Don't feel sorry for me. You asked me a question, I answered it. I don't want your pity."

Her eyes popped wider. "I'm sorry."

He huffed a frustrated breath. "No, don't apologize. I'm just trying to draw a line in the sand here. Don't pity me because of my childhood. Don't feel sorry for me or give me a different expectation because I didn't have parents. That's not helpful to me or anyone. I don't want you to like me just because I'm different. I don't want to be different."

She could see what she'd done. She'd victimized him, she'd felt sorry for him. How could he be her boyfriend — her partner, her equal — if she did that? "But Dax, you are different from anyone I've ever met. And I'm not talking because of your childhood. I'm talking about now."

The stone-tight tension in his face started to fade as he looked at her. "What do you mean?"

"You're a good man. You're thoughtful and considerate. You'd give the shirt off your back to someone in need. And you're smart and wise. You have a great outlook on life, and a strong faith in God. These are all very attractive qualities in you. I apologize for feeling sorry for you before. I won't do it again. I promise."

He gave her one firm nod, squared his shoulders and looked her in the eye. "Good."

"But it does explain to me why you've never been to the beach. So, let's call this trip to Pawleys Island your first beach vacation. We'll make it great. You'll of course stay beachfront, at my mom and Hank's house, you'll eat great meals either that my mom cooks, or we can eat in the awesome restaurant inside Tom and Marianne's beachfront inn. Tom and Marianne," she reminded him, "are Hank's daughter and son-in-law. They own the Seaside Inn and it has a wonderful dining room where they cook three meals a day from scratch for their guests. We'll walk the beach, we'll swim ... I hope you brought a swimsuit?"

He nodded.

"And since you're just doing the video with me, you'll have time to relax while I'm doing Emma's and Stella's photo shoots."

"I can help you."

"You enjoy the beach. I absolutely love the beach — any beach — but particularly Pawleys Island. It's ... it's like a little slice of my own personal heaven. I'm the happiest there. It's relaxing and it's soothing, and even my problems seem less important when I'm there. I want you to discover that, too."

"Well, if you put it that way, I'm game. I'm in a vacation frame of mind."

They packed their stuff in her car, and he slid behind the wheel and they took off. It was about a five-hour drive, but since Dax had already driven five hours today getting to Pittsburgh from Ithaca, they didn't plan to arrive until evening. That was all right. As far as Jasmine was concerned, her "working vacation" had started the minute he'd shown up on her doorstep.

They talked about everything. More stories from her childhood, more stories from his. They hit potentially taboo topics like politics and religion, and found that although they had some differences, their core beliefs were fundamentally similar. They talked about food and sports and hobbies and TV shows and books. Jasmine had never met a guy who was simultaneously immensely masculine, and incredibly easy to talk to. In her experience, the he-men she was generally attracted to physically, were quiet and reserved. She usually had to carry the ball of the conversation because they ran out of topics to converse on quickly. The guys she'd known who were fun and talkative and entertaining — she had no physical attraction to. They were either gay, or they were straight, yet slightly feminine.

Dax was the whole package.

They reached the island and Jasmine guided him to the Old Gray Barn. The house had a grand history for many families as it had been a vacation rental for probably fifty years, but it particularly had a legacy for her mother, whose family used to visit here when Leslie was a child. They loved it so much, they came back year after year. Her mom had cemented so many memories here. When her life fell apart early last summer — her husband's affair, Jasmine going to Paris for a summer internship, and her school year ending — an endless summer of pain and loneliness awaited her, until she decided to put her fate in God's hands and take a roadtrip. Nowhere particular in mind, just go where the Spirit led her.

The Spirit did lead her to many meaningful people and places during that roadtrip. But ultimately, it led her right here to Pawleys Island, back to the Old Gray Barn, and to a certain rugged, handsome handyman who was working on the old house between rentals. Hank.

Theirs was a fast-paced romance filled with love, prayer, and the healing of two broken hearts. God put the two of them together at that particular junction of both their lives, for a reason. It was obvious to anyone who was around the two of them and witnessed their love for one another. Jasmine couldn't be happier for her mom. The fact that she could now live in her favorite part of the country, was icing on the cake.

"Here we are. Just pull up here, under the house."

"Under?" Dax glanced over at her, his eyes wide. He was probably certain he'd misunderstood her.

"Yeah," Jasmine chuckled. "See? It's on stilts. The cars go underneath. It's almost like a garage."

* * *

They quickly grabbed their bags from the trunk and dashed up the wooden staircase leading to the front door. Without bothering to knock, Jasmine tried the door and finding it unlocked, she pushed her way in.

"Mom! Hank!"

They were just inside in the great room and as soon as Dax and Jasmine entered, they were on their feet, happy voices blending and melding in the room. Dax hadn't seen anything like it. Jasmine hugging Leslie, then pulling Hank into an embrace. Dax hung back, an uneasy smile on his face. Then, Jasmine's mom Leslie came over to him and pulled him into a hug. She leaned closer to him so he could hear her over the din of voices in the room, "Thank you so much for bringing her here safely. We're so excited to see you both."

He nodded and his smile grew more comfortable. "My pleasure."

Hank approached him and held a hand out to shake. "Great to see you again. Welcome."

"Thanks. Glad to be here. It's a first for me."

Jasmine came over and put her arm through his. "Can you believe Dax has never been to a beach before?"

The way she said it made him sound like an alien, but she hadn't meant it harmfully, and neither did her parents take it that way. All they did was insist that he go out back and experience it immediately. They all sat and kicked off their shoes, headed down a rustic staircase at the back of the house, and stepped onto the beach.

The sand was cool on his bare feet, but incredibly soft. He'd seen pictures of beaches before, but he'd never given any thought to how the sand would feel on his feet. He presumed it was a little rough, but not at all. Soft, cool, comfortable sand to sink his toes into. The chill sent a shiver through him, and Jasmine reached for his hand. "I'll keep you warm," she whispered and he smiled. They walked through at least fifty yards of sand, straight toward the water.

"It's too dark to walk very far, but I at least want you to get your feet wet," she said joyfully and Dax knew that she was in her happiest state of mind when she was at the beach.

Jasmine pulled him into the ocean up to his mid-calf. The sweeping sound of the tide going in and out was calming and soothing. It filled his ears with an immensity he'd never heard before. The water was chilly, but not uncomfortably so. He looked toward the house, and saw that Hank and Leslie had stayed on the shore, and they stood together, arms around each other.

"Have you ever tasted saltwater?" Jasmine asked.

"No."

Jasmine smiled. "Stick your finger in the water, then lick it. Don't drink it, because it is incredibly full of salt."

He did as she instructed and cringed when he tasted the salt on his finger. "Wow. Unbelievable."

"Yeah, so when we go swimming tomorrow, try to avoid opening your mouth underwater."

He laughed. She turned toward him and he reached an arm around her, pulling her close. When they shared a kiss, he could taste the intense saltiness on both their tongues. He absorbed the scents, the sounds and the movement of the ocean. "It's too dark to see well. I can't wait to see everything tomorrow in the light."

"We could get up early and see the sun rise. You'll never forget it."

They stayed out for a while before heading back to the house. They grabbed towels in the sun porch, wiped sand off their feet and legs, then settled inside on the couches in the main room. Jasmine chattered on about anything and everything, and Dax enjoyed watching her with her parents, his eyes roaming across each face. This was what a close-knit family was like. He'd observed some. He'd made friends in junior high and high school who had families like this, where kids could talk and their parents would laugh and encourage conversation. He'd been in a few foster families like this, and he'd yearned to stay longer. Wished and hoped deep inside himself that he wouldn't be reassigned, that he could at least pretend he was a part of it.

"So Dax," Hank said to him now, "Jasmine tells us you're a massage therapist. How's that going?"

"Good. I just moved to a new salon from my last one, so I'm back to building up a clientele. But it's work I enjoy, and it's nice to help people."

"You've got to have strong hand and arm muscles," Leslie said. "I try to massage Hank's shoulders when he gets home after working all day, and I can only last ten minutes, max."

He nodded. "Yeah, it takes some building up, just like any other muscle set. I'm used to massaging for an hour at a time, usually five or six times a day."

"Wow."

The conversation went on till well after midnight, at which time Leslie stood up and said, "I've got to call it a night. Emma, Marianne and Stella will be here at nine tomorrow. We figure you'll need to do fittings. Maybe some alterations. They've reserved as much time as you need them this weekend for the photos and the videos."

"Awesome, Mom." Jasmine stood and kissed her as she walked by. "Don't worry about us. Just tell me what rooms you want Dax and I in."

She turned and gestured to two bedroom doors off the great room. "Both of these are made up."

Jasmine nodded and turned to him to explain. "Besides the master bedroom here on the ground floor, there are three

146

other smaller bedrooms on this level, then two huge dormitory-style rooms upstairs."

"I'm sure I'll be comfortable wherever."

Leslie leaned over and kissed his cheek as she walked past him, and Hank waved his goodnights to both of them on his way out.

When all was quiet, Dax said, "They are so nice. You know how lucky you are to have them, right?"

"I sure do." She patted the seat beside her on the couch. "I also know how lucky I am to have you. Why don't you join me over here?"

He rose to his feet and covered the few steps to the couch and lowered himself beside her. She put her hands on his face and tugged. It didn't take much encouragement as he turned toward her and took her in his arms, landing his lips on hers. They were so soft and warm and inviting. He ran his hands up and down her back, then landed on her cheeks. His pulse was racing and he couldn't think of a single place he'd rather be right now.

Jasmine eventually pulled back, her breath coming a little heavier than usual, her chest heaving. "Whoa."

"Yeah." Time to take stock and get control of himself. Talk. That was probably a good thing to try right now. "Does your mom know about our, uh, relationship status?"

"Oh! Didn't I tell you? Yes, I told her a few nights ago. She was very complimentary."

"She was?" That pleased him.

"Yes. In fact, her quote was, 'he's a keeper.'"

He pulled her into him, not so they could start kissing again, but just because he wanted to feel her against him. He wanted to know she was his, that she was close by. "That means a lot," he murmured.

"You're one of the good guys, Dax."

"Thanks."

They sat for a nice few minutes, then Jasmine announced that they had an early morning. She pointed out his room, and the bathroom they'd share, and they called it a night.

Chapter Twelve

Morning in the Old Gray Barn started with the smell of pancakes cooking on the griddle, spreading its delicious aroma throughout the entire first floor. Dax couldn't think of a better alarm. He got out of bed, straightened his sheets and covers and dug some clean clothes out of his bag. He walked on bare feet to the bathroom, and finding it open, he went in and took a five minute shower. He'd found himself in the unwanted position too many times of oversleeping his alarm and discovering he had fifteen minutes to get to work. A five minute shower, an apple to eat in the car, and a shortcut, and he could make it by his first appointment. Just barely.

That was something he'd need to work on. A little less hectic start to the day.

Like today. It wasn't his work schedule making him race through his personal hygiene, it was his stomach growling at the aroma of the pancakes. He wiped a towel over his hair, leaving it to dry on its own. He had a little natural curl, and Jasmine seemed to like it that way, so he left it. He studied his chin in the mirror, found that he wasn't quite due for a shave yet, so he left that, too. Dress quickly in shorts and a tee shirt. Good to go.

He walked into the kitchen and Leslie got a great big smile on her face, making him remember her comment to Jasmine about him. He hoped she still thought he was a keeper after getting to know him better. But it sure made his heart warm to her, knowing that she probably knew his background, and had endorsed him as her daughter's boyfriend anyway.

"Good morning," he said.

She left the skillet and took a few steps to him, kissing him on the cheek and patting him on the shoulder. "Good morning," she said, returning to the pancakes. "I sure hope you're hungry. I know Hank is, so I figured with two men in the house, along with Jasmine and I, who have both been known to put away quite a few pancakes, I better make a big batch."

He chuckled. "Let me put it this way. The delicious smell woke me out of a sound sleep, and my stomach hasn't stopped growling since."

"Good to hear!"

Jasmine's mom was a petite lady, short blonde hair, who looked happy and comfortable in every situation. By contrast, Jasmine was taller and brunette, but with the same happy outlook on life.

Just as the thought of Jasmine entered his head, Jasmine herself entered the kitchen. He gazed at her and she came straight to him and gave him a kiss. In front of her mom. Who didn't flinch, just smiled and said, "Morning, sweetie."

"Hi, Mom. I wanted you to see these before we start today."

Jasmine had brought her portfolio of selected shots from his photo shoot on top of the mountain, and when she pulled them out, Leslie swooned and oohed and ahhed. It was a little weird standing there, watching the two ladies going crazy over photos of him. But of course, he reminded himself, they weren't commenting on him; more so the clothes he was wearing, and the capability of those particular shots to impress fashion professionals enough to offer her a job. He was just sort of the middle man.

They sat and ate, and Hank joined them, pouring himself a cup of coffee. Conversation darted across the table and the pancakes lived up to his hopes of flavor.

Before the meal was done, the front door opened and a small family – mom, dad and little girl – he assumed was Marianne, Tom and Stella, came in. Like Jasmine had the night before, they didn't wait to knock, they came in, then announced their presence.

"Hello, everyone, good morning, good morning," began Jasmine's stepsister, Marianne, but didn't get half her greeting out before her little daughter – Jasmine's step-niece, Stella – blew in with excited greetings for her family. She ran first to Hank, "Paw Paw, hi! I'm going to wear Jasmine's clothes and she's going to take pictures of me!"

"Yes, sweet pea, you'll be the prettiest little model there is, won't you?" the older man murmured to her while holding on tight.

Then she swung over to Leslie. "Grandma Leslie, will you watch the photo shoot?"

"Of course, sweetheart. We'll both be there."

Jasmine greeted Marianne and Tom, then grabbed Dax's arm and pulled him over. "Everyone, this is Dax, my boyfriend."

She said it with a beaming smile, which Marianne returned to her with a wink. Marianne welcomed him, gave him a quick hug and patted his shoulder, then Tom came over with a handshake and a few words. This family was all about affection and love, it was so obvious and inherent with all of them.

"Hello, pretty little girl," Jasmine said, squatting down to receive the full body slam hug of her step niece.

"She could barely sleep last night, she was so excited about being your model," Marianne said with a grin. "She hasn't been able to talk about anything else ever since I told her."

"Well, princess, you're doing me a big favor modeling for me. These pictures will help me get a good job in fashion. If I end up working for a children's clothing company, I'll get you free clothes."

Stella squealed.

"Come to my room and we'll try your outfits on."

* * *

Jasmine took Stella outside, onto the beach behind the Old Gray Barn. The rest of the family stayed on the sunporch, watching the progress of the photo shoot, but out of sight, so as not to distract Stella. Jasmine gazed through the viewfinder of her camera. These shots were going to be adorable. Stella was such a natural little beauty, and the fashions Jasmine had made for her enhanced the windswept beach look that was emerging in the frames.

Jasmine snapped a few shots as they walked to the water line. Stella wore a sundress in blue sea tones, one shade emerging seamlessly into the next in horizontal stripes from top to bottom. Placing her in front of the ocean waves, with a crystal blue skyline behind her would enhance the color scheme of the dress.

"Here you go, sweetie. For this photo shoot I don't want you to just stand and smile at the camera. I want you to do whatever feels natural. Smiles are fine, but also other expressions. If you see something on the beach that catches your interest, lean over and pick it up, study it, whatever. I guess I want you to forget that I'm here, taking pictures of you. Don't pose. Got it, sweetie?"

For only being five years old, and never having modeled before, she got it remarkably well. She did some "Say cheese!" poses, but then her natural curiosity got the better of her and Jasmine got some beautiful shots of her discovering shells, her airy dress blowing in the breeze, her long light brown hair falling over her face, her natural smile unhampered.

They did a few clothing changes. White pedal pushers with a blue navy style jacket. Peach shorts with a pastel multi-colored tank top. Jasmine took photos of her in front of the ocean, then turned so the beach house was in the background. For the last set of photos, she took Stella on the sunporch and took some shots with the rustic wood of the porch, and then for fun, some family shots of her with her parents and grandparents.

"How's it going?" Marianne asked.

Jasmine lowered her camera. "Done. She did great. I have hundreds to choose from. I'd be happy to put all the good ones on a CD and give it to you so you can develop those you want."

Marianne beamed. "I'd love that."

"Thank you so much for loaning me your beautiful little model. She did awesome."

As the family socialized, Jasmine went into her room and pulled up the results of her shoot onto her laptop. Dax joined her and they sat cross-legged on the bed, gazing at shot after shot, full screen.

"You got some great images. You're a very talented photographer."

She laughed. "Photography's not my thing. But in fashion, you need some basic skills so you can showcase your designs. No one's going to see what you can do unless you can present them in an attractive way."

"You've got so many. How do you narrow down to the best ones? You can't send a hundred shots with your job applications, right?"

"Yeah, that's the tough part. Picking out and presenting only the very best. Potential employers in the fashion industry are always busy and on a schedule. I have to be courteous of their time. If I send them a hundred photos, even if they were all wonderful, they'd probably cut me out of the running because I pissed them off."

He laughed.

"When I was doing yours," she continued, "I was ruthless with finding reasons to cut a photo out. A hair was out of place. Or a wrinkle in your pants was noticeable. Gone. On to the next." She looked over at him and smiled. "Who am I kidding? You're so camera-ready all the time, it was hard to find any flaws with you."

He gazed at her, his eyes darkening from cocoa-brown to ebony. His breath caught and he leaned in and rested his lips on hers. Her heart increased its rate and she clutched his shoulders, forgetting all about photos and fashions and models. Her whole world was the warmth of his mouth on hers.

"Thank you," he murmured.

She managed a casual laugh despite the racing of her pulse and breathing. "For the kiss?"

He settled back, leaning away from her on the bed, creating some distance as if on purpose. His chest heaved slightly and she admired the movement of the cotton covering his chest. "Well, that too. Always love your kisses. But I was thinking of, for including me in the family. They're amazing."

His words warmed her heart. "They are, aren't they? But you know it's a blended family. Mom and Hank are still newlyweds. I didn't even meet Marianne, and her brother Jeremy till about seven months ago. It's so different from my actual family – the one I grew up with – me, Mom and my dad."

"Different how?"

She thought about it. "I don't know, this group is much more boisterous and happy and open about their love and affection. My dad, well, you know how he is. Very responsible and mature and grown-up. I think somewhere along with the way he forgot how to have fun. My mom is ecstatic with Hank. Loves him to death. It's so obvious. But I think she lost the fun with my dad. I know they loved each other, but after all that time together, they lost the luster, I guess."

Dax nodded. "Sometimes family is the people you choose to love, not necessarily the ones that connect you by blood."

She took in his face, his beautiful smile, his intelligent eyes. "Who's the family you choose, Dax?"

His gaze dropped to the bedspread. He studied the pattern for a moment, then looked back at her. "A mishmash, really. Pedro is family, even though we don't have the same bloodlines. I love that kid and he loves me, too. We have a strong connection. And one of the foster moms I had, Carol, she made a big impression on me and my life. I lived with her and two other kids for nine months. It was a long time, relatively. She was the most generous and loving person I'd ever met. She opened her home to us, fed us, like other foster parents. But she was different. She loved us. She asked us about our day. Listened to our stories, gave advice when we needed it. I still remember some of the things she told me about growing up well and making a success of your life as an adult."

"She was like a mom to you."

"Sure was. I owe a lot to her."

"What happened to her? Do you stay in touch?"

"We did. It was time for me to move on. They reassigned me when I was seventeen. I kept her phone number and stayed in touch for three years. She died before I reached twenty one."

"How awful. What happened?"

"I never realized it because she never told me, or any of her other fosters. But she was fighting a disease the whole time I lived with her. I never thought about why she didn't work – she always took great care of us – but she had MS. They moved me on, along with the others, because she couldn't handle the demand anymore. Her disease had progressed where she couldn't move and function. She lived alone for a while, then they moved her into a facility. She died from it. I had just talked to her about two months before that and she never let on how much her life had changed. She just wanted to hear me talk. She wanted to know what was going on with me."

"What a wonderful woman."

"Yep. Carol. I was lucky our paths crossed. She made a difference."

Jasmine laid back on the bed, and Dax followed her, lying beside her with his head resting on her stomach. It was so peaceful and comfortable. She felt safe with him. She was invigorated by their mutual attraction, yet she didn't get that apprehensive, scary feeling she knew only too well, that came from fending off physical advances by guys.

The subject of family was interesting. She thought she'd grown up in the perfect family. Mom and Dad, she, their only child. They gave her everything she could ever want. Perfect home, friends, love, support. And yet, here she was with her new family – people she felt happy to be with, but she didn't even know them a year ago. Marianne and Jeremy were her siblings, definitely so. She loved them as she would've loved any natural sibling her parents might have given her.

And Dax. Although their relationship was new, she welcomed him to consider her family, his family. And they'd see where things went. The future looked bright.

* * *

The next day, they left the Barn early and drove over to the Seaside Inn, where Tom, Marianne, and Stella lived. It was a quaint boarding house-type hotel on the beach that housed about a dozen guest rooms, along with an apartment that served as living quarters for the small family. The Inn featured a large kitchen and dining room where they offered three meals a day to their guests. Marianne had hired two renowned chefs who split responsibility for the daily meals, and the Inn was known in the region for its excellent southern-cooking meals.

Recently, Marianne had introduced a new feature to the Inn: a dinner theater. Combining her love of theater with the need for increased income opportunities, Marianne produced a highly popular production of *The Music Man* right here in the Inn dining room. Offering three shows a week, on Friday, Saturday and Sunday nights, the show drew musical theater lovers not just from their current Inn guests, but from all over the island, as well as the surrounding Myrtle Beach area. The production was staffed with many volunteer adult and children actors from the community, but Marianne ensured quality by hiring experienced performers from the New York theater scene. The play's duo of Professor Harold Hill and Marian the Librarian were staffed with Tieg and Roxanne, two actors seeking a break from the hustle and bustle of the big city. Accepting their roles at a dinner theater in a sleepy beach town provided a way to continue performing, and earning income, while giving their minds and bodies a refresh from the Big Apple.

Jasmine parked in the sandy lot across the road. Carrying her garment bags, she and Dax made their way up the stairs of the Seaside Inn. "So this morning," she told him, "you're going to meet Jeremy and Emma. Emma's going to model my women's designs while I shoot her. After a lunch break, I'll take video of you, Emma and Stella doing runway modeling on the stage in the dining room. That way, I'll have both stills and video to submit."

He nodded. "And Jeremy is your stepbrother."

"Yes, and Emma is his new wife. They just got married a few months ago. They're looking forward to meeting you."

He frowned at her and she giggled at his suspicion. Of course word had gotten out that Jasmine had a new boyfriend so the family was coming out in full force to meet him.

She breezed through the door and grinned at the sight of Jeremy and Emma sitting on the couch in the great room. They rose to their feet and she pulled them into a three-way hug.

"Hi, hi, hi, you newlyweds. How's married life?"

Jeremy put a protective hand on Emma's lower back. "It's great. Can't imagine life being any better."

"And how's the store going?"

Emma smiled at her husband. "Business is booming. We got a great location that pulls in traffic and people are not only buying pieces off the floor, but they're placing custom orders. Keeps Jeremy busy."

"It's a group effort. Emma's considering quitting her job at the magazine so she can work there full-time."

"Oh, you two lovebirds." The two of them were so stinkin' cute with the adoring glances and not being able to keep their hands off each other. Jasmine rolled her eyes but was actually elated for them. Their relationship had not been an easy one, and they'd had more than their share of hardship to overcome. This couple was living proof that love was worth fighting for. They had hard-earned their happily ever after. "I have someone special for you to meet."

She gestured for Dax. "This is Dax Murphy, my boyfriend."

Emma held out a hand, took his, then squeezed their combined hands with her other. "Dax, so pleased to meet you."

"Nice to meet you."

"Jeremy and I loved the story about how you met. And after seeing some of the photos from your shoot, I was feeling a little intimidated about doing mine."

"Why?"

"You look like a professional model! Your shots are awesome."

"Well, thanks, but no. I was happy to help Jasmine out but modeling is definitely not in my wheelhouse."

"Speaking of modeling," Jasmine said, "I brought your outfits, Emma. Can we go somewhere to try them on and see if any alterations are needed?"

"Sure. We can probably go into Marianne and Tom's apartment."

Jasmine tiptoed to give Dax a kiss on the cheek. "Be right back, you guys." She and Emma walked past the Guest Desk and tapped on the door to the Muellers' living quarters. It swung open and Marianne stood there.

"Oh, you're here!"

"Could Emma use your bedroom to try these on? I can do quick alterations if needed."

"Of course. Come right in. In fact, I need to do some work behind the desk. Make yourselves comfortable. Let me know when you need Stella for the video."

"Will do. Thanks, Marianne." Jasmine smiled at her stepsister as she breezed by. She unzipped the garment bags and pulled out three garments for Emma. A formal evening gown in a yellow chiffon, with bling-bling silver straps and accent under the bust. A tailored business suit with gray slacks, white fitted V-neck sweater and waist-length jacket. And a casual miniskirt in blue denim, a plaid cotton blouse tied at the waist and leather cowgirl boots.

"I love these!" Emma enthused. She made quick work of trying them all on. Jasmine worked on adjustments with tape and pins, and an occasional needle and thread. It was all about making them fit for the photos and the video, not permanently.

As Jasmine worked on alterations, Emma said, "So ... you and Dax."

Emma looked over at her. They were both on the couch in Marianne's living room, Emma positioned sideways to face her. "Yes, me and Dax."

"He's *so* good-looking." Emma waved a hand in her face.

"He is, isn't he?" Emma giggled.

"Wow."

"But his looks aren't the only good thing about him." Jasmine looked back to her alterations and continued talking while sewing. "He's a good person, Emma. He amazes me every day with his kindness and gentleness. His views on things. The world and family."

"Oh, Jasmine. That's so wonderful." Emma leaned forward and put a hand over Jasmine's. "Are you guys serious about each other?"

Were they? Jasmine wasn't sure how to answer that. "It's too new to be serious. And we're long-distance, so it's not going to be easy. But we both want to give it a try."

"That sounds promising."

"Really, my first priority right now is getting a job. Hopefully in New York. Then we'll live only a couple hours from each other. And honestly, there's nothing keeping him in Ithaca. I mean, he doesn't have to live there. If things worked out between the two of us, he could move to New York, too." Suddenly she felt a jerk of discomfort. "But whoa, we're getting way ahead of ourselves. We've never even talked about him moving to where I find a job. I have no idea if he'd even want to. I'm just saying he's flexible. He's a masseuse. He could do that anywhere."

"Well, I think it's great. I've never met any of your boyfriends before. It's obvious you have very good taste."

"I haven't had a lot of boyfriends. In fact, I haven't been on a date in almost a year."

"What? You're kidding. A girl as pretty as you?"

"Really. I don't have much experience with guys. I'm a big flirt but I haven't had a steady boyfriend since way back in high school." Jasmine finished her work and set the garment aside. "In fact, I'm a little nervous that I'll mess things up, truth be told."

"What do you mean?"

Jasmine sighed. "I've never had an adult relationship before, you know? Dax is a grown man and I'm sure he's a lot more experienced than me. I'm not sure what to do when things get, you know, to a certain stage."

Emma studied her. "You mean, physically?"

"Yes," Jasmine breathed, relieved that she didn't have to spell it out for her.

Emma scooted closer to her. "You do what feels right to you. There are no wrong answers. If you don't want to do something, and Dax is pushing you, then you need to be honest with him and tell him no."

Jasmine nodded, looked down to her lap. "But what if that becomes an issue between us? He wants to, and I don't? What if that's something that he can't get past? You know, being a grown man and all."

Emma looked at her closely. "Sweetheart, have you ever …?"

Jasmine shook her head. "No. I'm a virgin. It's always been important to me to wait till I was married. But that's when I assumed I would be married right out of college. Like my mom and dad did. Doesn't look like that's going to happen."

"That's wonderful. And when you meet the right guy that you want to marry, it'll be important to him, too. Whether that's Dax or someone else."

Jasmine nodded. "But men have urges, I know. Sexual urges. How do I know if I'm being unfair to him? Teasing him without intending to? Or taking things too far before I say no?"

"The right man will respect you. It's all about communication, Jasmine. When the time comes, talk to Dax and tell him how you feel."

Jasmine studied Emma's face, unsure how she would ever talk to Dax about something this private, this personal. "You think so?"

"Yes. Not right now. But when the time is right, you be honest with him about your feelings, and ask him to respect your wishes. I bet he will not only understand, but will support you on it."

"He's a good guy."

"He seems like it. Now, don't worry. Be yourself and have fun."

Jasmine smiled and pulled her into a hug. "Thanks, sis. It's so great to have a sister to talk to."

Emma laughed. "I'm an only child, you know, just like you. I'm loving having sisters."

Jasmine pulled herself to her feet. "Okay, let's do this thing."

* * *

Dax watched Jasmine and Emma disappear into Marianne's apartment, then he turned his attention back to Jeremy. The

163

guy was looking at him, and glanced away when he was discovered.

"So, you own your own business?" Dax asked, making conversation.

"Yeah. I design and build wooden furniture, and I just opened a storefront for it."

"That sounds great."

"Keeps me busy." Both men sat in silence for a moment. "And you do massage?"

"Yep. It's a pretty good field. Easy to find work for licensed masseuses."

"That's good." Another pause. "So, how long have you and Jasmine been together?"

Dax shrugged. "Not long. She came in for a massage the weekend of her college graduation and I did it. That's how we met."

Jeremy nodded. "Yeah, I heard the story. Are you, uh, interested …? I mean, uh, what are your, uh …?"

Dax laughed. "Jeremy. Are you trying to ask me, what are my intentions toward your sister?"

Jeremy dipped his head and chuckled. "Yes. I guess I am. But I'm horrible at this. My one sister has been married for ten years, and my other one lives half a country away."

Dax studied him. "Do you feel protective of Jasmine?"

"You know it's crazy, but I do. Crazy because I haven't known her that long. My dad just married her mom less than a year ago. But that girl is special. From the first time I met her, she made me laugh. She's got a free spirit and she's got this optimism about the world. I'd sure hate for something … or someone … to break that."

Dax nodded. He'd sure hate that, too.

"But she's smart. Especially about people. I owe her, big time. There was a time I got into my head that I'd be doing Emma Jean a favor if I backed away from our relationship. I was doing the unselfish thing. Setting her free to find someone better for her, regardless of the fact that I loved her like crazy. Guess who was the only one brave enough and smart enough to step up to me, break through my stubborn determination and tell me the truth?"

"I'm guessing it's Jasmine."

"That's right. She told me I better not let the best woman I'd ever met get away from me. She told me in no uncertain terms that Emma and I should be together, and leaving her would be a huge mistake. Of course, she was right. And Emma and I were married about four months later."

Dax nodded.

"So forgive me a little bit the protective big brother routine. You treat her right. You treat her with respect. And everything will be fine between you and me."

He said it with a smile, and Jeremy didn't strike Dax as a violent man, but he was serious. He was getting his message across. Dax had to respect the man for making sure he knew it. And he sure was glad Jasmine had such a supporter in her corner. Dax held a hand out. "Message taken."

The two men shook.

Jeremy rose to his feet. "I understand we're double dating for dinner tonight or tomorrow. Meanwhile, nice to meet you, and I got to get back to the store."

Chapter Thirteen

The photo shoot with Emma went well. Emma had a natural talent. She not only was stunningly beautiful with a slim figure and a mountain of brunette curls on her head that bounced with her every move, she moved well and looked great in clothes. Jasmine understood the value of a good model in accentuating the beauty of her clothes, and despite the fact that none of her models were professional, she could not have picked a better trio for her portfolio.

When she'd once again snapped off over a hundred photos, she called a break. Walking toward Emma in the cool white sand, she called, "Great work, Emma. I'm thrilled with all of these. I'll make sure you get the good ones. Maybe you can make a photo collage for that man who is head over heels for you."

Emma's face transformed into a shy smile and Jasmine detected a hint of a blush.

"You guys are so in love, aren't you?"

"Yes, we are. I never knew it could be like this. Out of disaster came something beautiful and I thank God every day for putting Jeremy and me together."

Jasmine brushed her hand over Emma's shoulder, and thought briefly of the last few months they'd endured together. Emma's father, a crazy man with a vendetta, had kidnapped Stella, befriending her under a false identity. He lured her into a car, took her out into some isolated woods where luckily, smart little Stella escaped. Search and rescue volunteers from three surrounding counties searched for nine hours, culminating with the thrill of Emma and Jeremy finding the little girl, and delivering her home to her terrified parents.

Emma had to cut ties with her evil father, who was whisked away to jail, and she convinced her overly loyal mother to do the same. Repairing her friendship with Marianne and Tom was a challenge, despite the fact that Emma had no idea what her father was brewing up. But fortunately, her and Jeremy's relationship blossomed amidst all the ugliness, and they got married just a few short months ago.

Jasmine gave her a warm hug. "How about we reconvene here at the Inn at two o'clock for the video? I'd like to spend a little time with Dax and show him what it is I love so much about the beach."

They made their way back into the Inn and the dining room smelled of something wonderful. Marianne bustled out of the kitchen. "Welcome, welcome! Lunch is being served. Do you guys want to take a table? Or, if you'd rather, I could pack a picnic and you could take it down on the beach."

Jasmine smiled. "You read my mind. I wanted to spend some beach time with Dax."

Marianne grinned. "Say no more," she said and made an about face back into the kitchen.

Jasmine wandered into the great room, then into the sun porch, searching for him. There he sat on the screened-in porch, his feet up on an ottoman, glancing at a magazine on his lap. She came up behind him and wrapped her arms around his shoulders, leaning in and placing a kiss on his cheek. He leaned back into her and his cheeks popped with the smile that covered his face.

"Hi, baby," he murmured.

"Hi back." She came around to the front of him and lowered herself onto his lap. He wrapped his arms around her and pulled her tight. "Are you bored stiff?"

"Of course not. How'd the shoot go?"

"Great. I can't be more pleased with all the shoots. I have some great material to start sending out next week."

He lifted a finger and ran it gently across her face. She shivered. "Next is the video?"

"Yeah. But not yet. I set that for 2:00. We've got some time now to go to the beach."

"Sounds good." They got up and walked to the car, where they pulled a bag full of swim suits and towels out of the trunk. They borrowed a couple unoccupied guest rooms to change and met back in the great room. When Dax sauntered in wearing a loose-fitting Ocean Pacific suit and nothing else except a pair of flip flops, Jasmine sucked in a breath.

The man was a vision of masculine beauty.

Fearing she was staring, she said, "Okay, it's settled. I need to design a line of men's swimwear next." She was kidding, but only half so. Spending hours taking photos of him wearing swimwear, gleaming in his healthy fitness, would be her idea of a good time.

Meanwhile, he had his own case of speechlessness. His eyes took in her two-piece – a modest sports bra-type top, and high-waisted bottom – and she could see the appreciation form on his face. "You look great," he said.

"Thanks," she returned, her voice breathless.

Marianne broke the spell between them by walking into the great room, carrying a picnic basket. "Here you go, guys. Everything you could want for a lunch on the beach."

Dax ogled the basket, filled to overflowing. "Wow, you didn't have to go to that much trouble, Marianne."

Jasmine laughed. "I've heard all about your famous picnic baskets, Marianne. There's probably enough to feed a family of five in there, right?"

Marianne laughed. "No trouble at all. The chefs make the food for our guests. I just grabbed some and stuck it in here for you." She waved with a smile. "Have a good time, you two."

Dax hefted the basket and they walked down to the sand. They turned at the water line and strolled about ten minutes. Jasmine opened the basket and pulled out a red and white checkered table cloth and spread it out on the sand. "Want to take a swim first?" She frowned at him. "Do you know how to swim?"

He nodded.

She lowered the bag of towels on the cloth, and he lowered the basket. They joined hands and walked toward the water. On the way, strips of sand sparkled in the sunlight. Jasmine pointed it out. "This is bits of seashell ground into a thin powder by the tide and when hit by the sun, it's almost like glitter sprinkled on the sand."

He bent over at the waist to study the phenomenon. "Beautiful."

They walked a bit further and Jasmine pointed again. "See these holes in the sand? Those holes are where a mollusk dug in for the night. Now that it's morning they'll dig to the top and leave a trail behind them as they crawl." She looked around. "Oh, look, here's one."

He came over and saw a long tubular shell in the midst of a two-inch trail of white sand. "That shell is alive?"

"Yes," Jasmine said with a smile. "He's in there and he has one little foot-like thing that he uses to push himself around."

Dax stuck a finger in the mollusk's direction and brushed over the fleshy part sticking out of the shell. The creature immediately pulled back into its spot of protection. "So cool."

They made it to the water's edge. Being early in the season, the water was brisk and cool. The waves were never big in this part of the beach, but today it was calm as a plate of glass. They walked in about waist-high and then Dax, without warning, dove under. Jasmine squealed. He surfaced, the sun catching droplets of sea water dripping from his long locks.

"Feels great," he said, his smile reaching out and touching her heart.

Not to be outdone, Jasmine gathered her courage and dove under, too. After a moment of shock at the cold, she settled into her normal infatuation with the sea. Dax made his way over to her and brushed her hair back from her face. She gripped him by the shoulders and brought her legs up, wrapping them around his waist. They stood there in each other's arms, surrounded by the water.

"I see why you like the ocean so much."

Jasmine's heart gave a little thrill. "Oh, I'm so glad you like it. I was sort of fearing that I'd get you out here and you'd hate it."

"What's to hate?"

"I don't know, but not everyone communes with the ocean. I didn't grow up here, but some of the happiest moments in my life took place on some beach. My mom feels the same way; she and I are alike in that way. Which is one of the reasons I'm thrilled for her that she gets to live here permanently now."

He pulled her closer and kissed her. The warmth generated by their joined lips formed a tantalizing contrast with the chill surrounding their bodies. Dax's fingers explored the bare skin on her back, underneath the strap of her suit top. She allowed her fingers to wander across his bare back.

He tore his lips from hers and a shiver ripped through his upper body.

"Are you cold?"

He snorted. "I don't think that's what the shiver was from."

"What do you mean?"

He clamped his mouth shut with a smirk. "You make me shiver, girl."

She laughed.

"Serious. You make me feel … good."

She knew what he meant. It was hard to put into words, but she felt the same way. He made her heart race. Being near him gave her body a physical reaction. It was chemistry. He made her blood cascade through her veins.

And he evidently felt the same.

"You make me feel good, too." She left it at that, happy with the discovery. Eventually they made their way back to their picnic spot and enjoyed a feast.

* * *

A few hours later, they were in the dining room at the Inn, shooting the video. All three models had selected their personal favorite outfit from their own collection. Jasmine set them up on the *Music Man* stage, simulating a Paris catwalk. She wasn't exactly sure what the end product would look like, but at least her potential fashion employers would see her designs in motion.

She filmed each model walking back and forth solo, then she filmed the three of them walking together, sort of like a small family. She had gathered about eight minutes of video total. She'd have to add some background music when she got home.

She took a last look at the small gathering on stage when a voice beside her said, "What's going on up there?"

Jasmine turned and faced a beautiful blonde woman. The phrase "All American Girl" came immediately to mind. She could picture her riding a horse on a farm, her blonde ponytail sweeping out behind her, her skin a healthy tanned glow.

Jasmine held her hand out. "Hi. I'm Jasmine."

"I'm Roxanne."

"Oh, the actress!"

"That's right. Marian the Librarian, at your service."

Jasmine laughed. "I'm borrowing your stage. I'm Leslie's daughter?"

"Oh, right. So, that makes you Marianne's sister, right?"

"Stepsister, but yes. I'm looking for a job in fashion and I've spent the last three weeks designing, sewing, and taking pictures of these guys modeling my clothes. Last step is a video. Hopefully it'll pay off soon with a job offer."

Roxanne gazed back at the trio, now casually chatting to each other. "Those clothes look great. And the models are good. You've got talent."

"Thanks. I just graduated from Cornell in Fashion Merchandising. I'm dying to start my career."

"Where do you want to work?"

"Anywhere with a paycheck. But ideally, New York."

Roxanne smiled. "I live in New York."

"Really? What are you doing here?"

Her eyes wandered away from Jasmine's, darted around the room, then back. "Long story. But let's just say, if you let it, New York will chew you up and spit you out. It's the best city in the world, but the worst, too. I am an actress. I need to be either there or LA. But I needed a reprieve, a break from the rat race. I turned down a pretty good off-Broadway job when this dinner theater gig came up. It was just what I needed for a little while – right when I needed it."

Jasmine was sure there was way more to this story than Roxanne was revealing, but it was none of her business, and everyone was entitled to their secrets. "I'm glad you could come to Pawleys Island. It's magical here, in so many ways."

"I agree with you. I'm starring in one of my favorite classic musicals of all time, I'm spending a lot of relaxing downtime in one of the most beautiful beach towns in the world, and I'm building my strength back to return to New York. Other than dealing with my irritating co-star," she said with a grim smile, "life couldn't be better."

Hmmm, interesting. "There's a story there."

Roxanne smirked. "Way more than I can get into in civilized company."

Jasmine liked her, in spite of the mystery. "Well, despite the irritations, I'm happy for you." She called up to Dax,

Emma and Stella. "That's a wrap, guys. Go ahead and get changed. If you want to keep any of the clothes, they're yours for the taking."

Stella squealed.

"So," Roxanne continued, "I know someone in the fashion industry. I'd be happy to connect the two of you."

Jasmine gasped and looked at her, wide-eyed. "You're kidding."

"No. I'm not saying she's someone with a lot of clout or anything, but she's working as a designer at Henderson-Cloy, and they have several fashion subsidiaries. She's a designer in their theater costuming line. They have contracts with most of the Broadway theaters. They also have a line that does retail."

"Oh, my gosh. That's exactly what I want to do. Live in New York City and work in the fashion industry. I don't care where. Does she love it?"

"Yes, she seems to. I mean, it's long, crazy hours. Deadline-driven. But she's working in her field. She has aspirations to open her own line of fashion but for now, she's happy working for a company while she builds her own portfolio. If you want me to reach out with an introduction, I'd be happy to. We were sorority sisters at New York University. We get together pretty often when I'm there."

"Oh Roxanne, that would be awesome. I'm so grateful. Thank you so much."

"Pay it forward, isn't that what they say? Your sister rescued me when she offered me this job. Now, you need a leg up to find your first job. I can see you're talented. You just need a little help getting started."

They exchanged phone numbers and email addresses, and Roxanne provided the name of this friend, Tessa Moore. "I'll send her an email of introduction, cc you, and then you can Reply all to forward her your photos and video. Who knows? She might be able to help."

"Thank you so much. I need all the help I can get."

The rest of their time on Pawleys sped by. Dax and Jasmine went out to dinner with Jeremy and Emma Jean. Jasmine had loved her stepbrother since the first time she met him, and now she cherished the chance to get to know her new sister-in-law a little better. Dax fit right in, developing an easy rapport with Jeremy and Emma. They shared crab legs, beers and laughs as they sat outside at a casual, wooden floored shack.

After their evening out, back at the Barn, Jasmine pulled her mother aside in the kitchen. "Can I talk to you a second?"

"Of course." Leslie wiped a crumb from the counter, then gave her daughter her full attention.

"I'm sorry if this is none of my business, or if it'll make you feel uncomfortable."

Leslie's eyebrows went up. "Uh oh."

Jasmine let out a breath. "Remember in the ER, and Dad asked if you could forgive him for his transgressions, and you said no, but you'd pray on it?"

Leslie's only response was a narrowing of her eyes. Jasmine rushed on, "Look, I fully get why you wouldn't be ready to forgive him for being unfaithful and breaking your heart. But as the daughter of both of you, I just wanted to put my two cents in. Take it or leave it."

She waited for some invitation from her mom. Seeing she wasn't going to get one, she continued, "Living with him the last few weeks puts me up close and personal with his life as it is now. How empty it is of love and family. It's not that I feel sorry for him. I know he brought it all on himself. But I see how happy you and Hank are, surrounded by love and laughter and I just see a big contrast. And I think Dad's learned something from all this. I think he's regretful, and he realizes he messed up and can't fix it. But he's trying to be a better person."

Leslie stared at her so long, Jasmine almost turned away. Then her mom lifted a hand and laid it on Jasmine's cheek. "It's very, very sweet of you to try to help him."

Jasmine shrugged. "I'm not trying to help him, I guess I'm just putting in a good word for him. For what it's worth."

Leslie's mouth curled into a grim smile. "I did pray about it. Many times. I've prayed for the ability to forgive and release the anger. God's working on me. Maybe this is another way He's getting the message across."

Jasmine liked the sound of that. The thought that she was in tune enough with God to deliver His message, pleased her.

The next morning, Leslie made them bacon and cheese omelets. Hank delayed the start of his work so he could spend time with them in the morning before they left. Jasmine took her second cup of coffee to her room so she could pack her suitcase. Her mom came into the room behind her.

"We're so glad you came to visit, sweetie."

"Me, too. Nothing like a beach fix. I wish I could stay, but Dax has appointments scheduled tomorrow. I wouldn't ask him to reschedule them, and he's got to get all the way back to Ithaca tonight."

Leslie nodded. "You're welcome to come on back after you get all your applications submitted. If you get a job right away, you probably won't have a vacation for some time."

Jasmine laughed. "That's good incentive. Wouldn't it be awesome if Roxanne's friend helped me secure a job with her company?"

"It sure would. Regardless of whether she can or not, it can't hurt having a contact in the Big Apple."

Jasmine zipped up her suitcase and rolled it to the door. Her mom caught her arm and squeezed it. She winked. "I like him," she said in a near whisper.

Jasmine smiled. "I do, too."

* * *

Before she wanted to accept it, they were back at her dad's house in Pittsburgh, standing in front, arms wrapped around each other, saying good-bye. Jasmine held back her tears. She didn't want him to see them, and she didn't want to be the kind of woman who cried when her boyfriend wasn't around. But their long-distance arrangement was so hard. She had no idea when she'd see him again.

She pressed herself as close to him as possible, his arms wrapped around her, and his hands clasped at her back. She breathed in and took comfort in the familiarity of his scent and warmth.

"What are your plans?"

"Work like crazy starting tomorrow, finalizing the shots, editing the video. Send everything out to the employers asking, then broaden my search to other employers I haven't applied to yet."

He looked down at her, his smile a beacon in the darkness. "Sounds like a plan, sweetheart. My smart, ambitious lady." He placed a soft, sweet kiss on her lips. "I'm proud of you."

She laid her head against his chest. It pained her to say it, but, "You better hit the road, baby. It's still a long drive for you."

"Yeah."

He pulled her into a long kiss, her heart racing, her breath hitching. When he drew back, she stepped up on the curb, and watched him get into the car. Holding back her tears, she held a hand up as he drove away.

* * *

Dax drove north as the last of the daylight surrendered and the darkness began to overtake. It had been a great weekend, a weekend of milestones. He'd experienced the ocean for the first time. Walking on the sand, observing the wildlife, swimming in the waves. He wished he'd had the chance to do it all before now. But now was good enough. And, as an added bonus, his first time was with Jasmine.

Jasmine, in her two-piece swimsuit accentuating her trim, fit physique. It had been an effort to restrain himself from staring, open-mouthed, when she first emerged, showing all that skin. His imagination ran away with images of running his fingers down that soft, tan skin; satin, perfect skin encasing glowing, gleaming curves.

Jasmine.

He gripped the steering wheel and concentrated on taking a deep breath in, pushing it out.

His phone rang and he fumbled to pull it out of his back jeans pocket. He glanced at the caller, intending to throw it on the seat beside him. But it was Pedro. He'd take a minute. He pressed Speaker.

"Hey Pedro. What's up?"

"Hi. How was the beach?"

"Unbelievable. Have you ever been to one?"

"No."

"This was my first. So glad I went." He began to describe the texture of the sand on his feet, the saltiness of the water on his tongue, the coolness of the waves against his skin. Pedro wasn't having it.

"So what about the girl?"

"The girl?"

"Yeah, man. Jasmine."

Dax smiled. "We had a good time. A real good time."

"She's something special, huh?"

"Yeah." He answered automatically, with no regard to the ribbing and teasing that admission would surely bring from the thirteen-year-old on the other end.

"Jasmine and Dax sitting in a tree?" Pedro said with a laugh.

"Shut up."

"Seriously man, are you in lo-o-o-ve?" He drew out the word comically.

Dax started to deny it because it seemed the thing to do, the thing that was called for in a conversation with a juvenile. But he stopped.

Love. Was it possible?

He'd barely known Jasmine for a heartbeat. Could he be in love with her? He didn't have experience in that realm. He'd been "in like" with girls before. He'd certainly been "in lust." But with Jasmine, it was different. She was special. Sure, she was beautiful and he had a strong physical attraction to her. But she had potential for something more, something more lasting and permanent.

But how do you explain that to an immature adolescent?

"I don't know, buddy. Maybe."

The kid laughed and they talked a few minutes about Pedro's day, the progress of his finals and his plans for the summer. Then they said good night.

Chapter Fourteen

Jasmine awoke, anxious to get to work. She needed to edit her video into a few minute clip featuring all her fashions. She needed to go through all the photos she'd taken at the beach and narrow them down to a manageable number of only the finest photos. If she got all that done, she could start responding to the employers who had asked for these deliverables, and then expand her search to others.

Sounded like at least a week's worth of work.

First thing's first. She'd been away from email and social media while she was at Pawleys Island, so she needed to get reconnected. She took her cup of coffee, booted her laptop while sitting at the kitchen island and waited.

The whirring of the hard drive ensured her the thing was waking up after a short vacation. She sipped and daydreamed. Then, ding, ding, ding – little musical sounds filled the air. She pulled her mind back to the computer. Why was it going crazy?

Notifications. Lots of them. Hundreds. What was going on? What was all this stuff?

She looked at her loading Inbox. Notifications from Facebook and Twitter saturated it, filling the list, loading more and more. She switched to her internet browser, pulled up all her social media sites and studied her most recent posts.

There it was. Her posts about the Phone Booth Baby. They'd gone viral!

The Facebook post had been shared over a hundred times and it had almost five hundred comments. Good Lord. Her pulse raced, and she was unsure if she should feel excited or shamed by the results.

She clicked quickly over to Twitter. It had been retweeted forty seven times and had almost a hundred replies.

Her plans for productivity with her photos and job applications were immediately put on hold. She would have to dig into this phenomenon. What the heck was going on?

Her father walked by on his way to the coffee pot. He was dressed impeccably as always in his suit pants, white button down shirt and tie. "Hitting it bright and early, huh?"

"Yeah." Impulse had her wanting to hide what she was looking at from her dad. They'd talked briefly last night about her results from her trip, and he was very supportive of continuing with her job applications. This detour would not be well-accepted.

"Good job, honey." He came up behind her and planted a kiss on the top of her head. Jasmine surreptitiously pushed the laptop closed. "Put yourself on a schedule and get those things out."

"Yes, Daddy." She watched him grab a banana, put coffee in a travel mug, and head for the door. "Have a good day."

In the solitude of the empty condo again, she pulled open the laptop and dug into the amazing results of the post. A twinge of apprehension invaded her. No one she'd shared this endeavor with, supported it. Her mother wanted her to forget it. Dax had told her the same thing. Why was she so intent on pursuing it?

She paused, her eyes skimming over all the comments. It was tempting to find out if there was one helpful clue in there. How could she ignore them now? What harm could come from finishing the research she'd started? She blew out a breath and made up her mind. Kissing her hopes of a productive morning of job hunting good-bye, she dove into her Inbox.

After several hours of work, she'd disregarded all the comments wishing her good luck in her search, telling her they'd been to Pittsburgh once, and the ones sharing their own adoption stories. The weaning out had resulted in several potentially helpful comments.

One said, "Paul Mason was my next-door neighbor during this timeframe. I remember the day he found the baby and delivered her to the hospital because he was so excited when he came home, gushing with smiles and stories of the good deed."

Jasmine's pulse bumped up. That was the closest hit she'd had yet. She clicked on the person's name who had written the comment: Elisa Smith. Elisa's personal page came up. She still lived in Pittsburgh, was in her late fifties and posted all kinds of pictures of three particular young girls. Probably grandchildren. Jasmine opened up a Private Message box and typed, "Thank you for your response about Paul Mason. Do you have any further information about him? Is he on Facebook? Or could I contact him directly?"

She sent the message into cyberspace and went back to reviewing the list of comments. Moments later, her computer gave her a ding. Elisa had responded. She pulled up the note and read: "Unfortunately, Paul passed away several years ago. Such a nice man. Thanks for the memories. The thought of Paul doing this kind deed for a baby in need is so consistent with the man's character. I like the thought of his legacy being relived this long after it happened. God bless you, dear."

Jasmine sighed as she stared at the message. She gave a quick prayer of thanks for kind people who performed deeds every day, not knowing what impact they would have on the lives of others. Positive, generous deeds, not for the recognition or the reward, but because they knew it was the right thing to do.

God's network of people, helping each other, one step at a time.

She continued through the other messages. Maybe one would help her take a step further.

Almost an hour later, she ran across an intriguing comment. "Contact me by Private Message. I may have information you'd be interested in."

Jasmine tried to tamp down her excitement. Could be a whacko with no information whatsoever. On the other hand, it could be something useful. She clicked on the woman's name: Fran Chambers, pulled up a Private Message box and typed, "Hi. I'm the one who posted about the Phone Booth Baby. You asked me to contact you?"

Hoping for an immediate response from Fran proved futile. Would someone named Fran have Instant Messenger on her smart phone, able to respond on the spot to her message? In her mind, she didn't imagine Fran to be particularly tech-savvy. Jasmine sat and stared at the Private Message, willing Fran, wherever she was, whoever she was, to respond.

Fifteen minutes of waiting got sucked into a vacuum of inactivity, a total waste of time. Jasmine glanced at the clock on the stove. She'd been at this Phone Booth Baby thing now for three hours. She'd reviewed all the comments, followed up with the few that held promise of more information. This last message to Fran was the best lead she had. And Fran wasn't talking. So, she needed to move on.

She dragged herself away from the computer and jumped on her dad's treadmill. She set the pace to a brisk jog for a half hour. She pushed herself faster and faster, and when she was done, her heart was pumping a rewarding pace, her skin was moist with perspiration and she felt better about sitting around like a slug all morning.

She needed to focus on the photos for the rest of the day. No more Phone Booth Baby distractions. If Fran happened to respond, that was a different story. But otherwise, all work, all day.

Late afternoon, she received a text from her dad: "I'll eat at the office. You're on your own for dinner." Jasmine smiled, stretched her arms over her head and yawned. She'd been on her own for dinner for the last four years. Yet her father felt compelled to tell her today that she needed to dig up her own food. Like she would starve if he didn't come home and feed her.

Ahh, she was being too hard on him. They were more roommates now than father/daughter. He was just being courteous. They'd gotten along fine since graduation, she and her dad. As long as they didn't scratch beneath the surface and talk about the White Elephant in the room: his mid-life crisis, his affair and destruction of his marriage. No, as long as they didn't talk about that, they were fine.

Their living arrangement was temporary at best. She'd either move to New York to work in the fashion industry, or, if she was unable to secure a career, and she just needed to take a job to make money, she'd move to live with her mom. No brainer.

Thinking about the beach led her to think about Dax. She smirked. Actually, just about anything led her to think about Dax these days. She glanced at her phone, wondering if he was done with his clients for the day. She'd take a risk and call him, see if she could brighten his day, or him hers.

He answered after three rings. His deep, hushed voice caused a rumble in her lower stomach. "Hi. Are you with a client?"

"No, just finishing up. Good timing." He was speaking softly and she could picture him in the hallway outside his massage room, not wanting to disturb the client he'd just finished, with their immersion back out of the paradise he'd put them in with his magical fingers. "How's your day going?"

She took a deep breath, let it out. "Busy. Sedentary. I finished editing the video. I might send it to you and get your take on it."

"Great."

"And I'm done selecting Stella's photos. Just have Emma's left. I'll tackle that tomorrow. Then I'll be ready to start sending stuff out."

"Not a bad day's work."

"Well, I got distracted. My Inbox exploded while I was gone."

"Really? With job offers from New York?" He laughed.

"No. With my social media posts that went viral."

He paused. "What social media posts?"

"Before I left for Pawleys I whipped off a couple posts asking for help on the Phone Booth Baby case. I hoped they would go viral, but I never had any expectation that they would. But they did! They really did!" He didn't respond and she wondered if she'd lost the connection. "Dax?"

"Yeah." Was his voice hushed because his client had walked by? "Why are you doing this, Jasmine?"

"Doing what?"

"This is a mistake. This is exactly what I was talking about when I was sharing my concerns about the two of us being together."

Her breath was coming shorter now. "What?"

"You have an abundance of family members, Jasmine. Lots of good people who love and support you. And yet, it's not enough. You're grasping on to this one mystery woman who abandoned your mother nearly fifty years ago. For some reason, you can't let it go. Are you ever satisfied with what God has already provided you? Or, do you always want more?"

The harshness of his words made her tongue-tied for a moment. Her mind whirled and she finally put her thoughts together. "But why? What's wrong with wanting God's blessings in abundance? Let's see, I think it's in Matthew, the Bible says, Seek and you shall find. Knock and the door will be opened. Ask and it shall be given. To me, that means that God wants to give us our heart's desire. Or, at least to go after it. Sure, we don't get everything we want. But that's no reason not to try."

There was a pause from Dax. She guessed she could understand why he was so adamant on this point. It struck so close to home with his own family situation. Maybe he was taking it too personally.

"I think you need to respect your mother's wishes on this, Jasmine. I think this is headed for disaster."

"What I'll do is tell my mom what I've come up with, and let her give me the green or red light to continue. Okay?"

He hesitated, then said softly, "So what did you get?"

"On the post?"

"Yeah."

"A lot of Shares. A lot of comments. Very little of importance. I did get a note from the neighbor of Paul Mason who rescued my mom from the phone booth and took her to the hospital. She said he was a nice guy, and she remembered the day he discovered my mom. He was happy to help her."

"That's nice."

"Yeah, a real Good Samaritan type. But I can't get in touch with him personally. He's dead."

"Okay."

"But my last lead is from a woman named Fran. She didn't give me any information, but she left a comment telling me she had information, and asking me to contact her privately. Which I did. Now I'm waiting to hear from her." His quietness left a sense of ill-boding in her.

His sigh reached her across the cellular network. "I just wish you wouldn't mess with this, Jasmine. This isn't your battle to fight. This is your mom's history, and she doesn't want to pursue it. So why are you? Why do you want to dig up a can of worms?"

She gripped the phone tighter. "It's my family, too. This is my grandmother we're talking about. If I can find her, why wouldn't I give that some effort?"

"She doesn't want to be found."

"How do you know?"

"Because she hasn't reached out to your mom. It would be so much easier for her to find your mom, than for you to track her down. Haven't you considered that at all? She's either embarrassed or ashamed. Or she just doesn't care. She made her decision and has moved on."

Jasmine hesitated. Was he right? She was determined to satisfy her curiosity. What could it hurt? The worst that could happen would be, she found the woman who'd abandoned Leslie, and she refused to speak to Jasmine. Okay. She'd deal with it.

On the other hand, the best that could happen is she'd find her birth grandmother, who would welcome her and Leslie with open arms. Her birth grandmother might not be savvy with the details of finding someone, and had just chosen the path of sitting back and praying for God to lead her daughter to her. If so, maybe God was working through Jasmine to answer those prayers.

She didn't know why, but she felt compelled to continue. Nothing this intriguing had ever happened to her in her lifetime.

Dax continued, "What's in the past is in the past. It doesn't define your future. People rise above mistakes of the past all the time. It's better to leave it alone."

"I see what you're saying. Thanks for your advice." And in that very nice, polite way, Jasmine closed the subject and went on to others. Twenty minutes later, she hung up and went to the kitchen to dig up some dinner.

Chapter Fifteen

The next few days flew by for Jasmine. She finished her job search deliverables and sent them out to those employers that had requested them. She also researched more fashion industry employers in New York, and sent them her materials as well. She corresponded with several of her college friends who had landed jobs, or were searching for jobs, and they shared leads with each other.

She also pointedly ignored the fact that Fran Chambers had not responded to her Private Message.

Whenever she started fixating on Fran, she allowed herself a moment or two, then she pushed herself to do something more productive.

On Thursday, she scanned her email list and selected one to open. She read the short message and she screamed. Full volume, top of her lungs scream. Of course, no one was there to hear it since her dad was in surgery. So she ran for her phone and dialed her mother. It went to voicemail. "Call me!" she said and called Dax. It went to voicemail. "Call me!"

She did an excited twirl in the living room, barely able to contain her adrenaline. Fortunately, her phone rang. It was her mom. "Mom!" she yelled. "I got an interview request in New York!"

"Oh, sweetheart! Good for you! This is the start of it! They loved your photos and your designs and you're going to start making your dreams come true."

She absolutely loved her mom, saying just the right words that she wanted to hear at this moment. She took a closer peek at the email. "Oh! Guess what. The interview is with Henderson-Cloy. This must be connected to the contact Roxanne made for me. You know, the actress at Marianne's dinner theater!"

"Oh, fantastic. You should call her."

"I will. In fact, I will right now."

"Okay, sweetie. Congratulations and keep me posted."

She disconnected on her mom and looked up her new contact number for Roxanne.

"Hello?" The sound of distant static came over the line. It took a moment for Jasmine to realize it was ocean surf.

"Roxanne? It's Jasmine Malone. You know, Marianne's stepsister."

"Of course! The fashion mogul."

Jasmine chuckled. "Yes, and I want to thank you. You evidently made an impression on your friend, Tessa. I got an interview request from Henderson-Cloy."

"Wow! That was fast. But hold on here. It wasn't me who made an impression on Tessa. It was you. When I sent you her email address, you sent her your photos and video. When she reviewed them, she called me. She was raving. They evidently have an opening in their Broadway division. They are shorthanded and don't have a huge budget. They need to hire a newbie without much experience – they can't afford an established name right now. But it's been so long since they've recruited straight out of college, they had no idea where to start. Then we placed your wonderful portfolio right into Tessa's hands. If she could've kissed me long distance, she would've."

Jasmine felt faint. "I don't know what to say."

"I do! Tell them you'll be there ASAP to interview. And tell them you're the perfect one to fill their opening. In fact, you'll barely need to tell them. Your photos speak for themselves. Good job, girl. The Big Apple is waiting for you."

Her head was spinning and she forced herself to sit down and think. Her eyes roamed over the email again. "Okay, whoa, whoa, whoa. Slow down. I should probably call Tessa. But her name's nowhere on this email."

"Sure. Give her a call; maybe she'll give you some pointers."

Jasmine gulped a deep breath. "Roxanne. Thank you. So much."

"Pay it forward, baby. Go forth and prosper. Meanwhile, I'll go back to my sunbathing."

* * *

The interview was set. Jasmine called Tessa, thanked her for the help, and listened to all kinds of tips about the company, the type of work, the interviewers, their expectations. Armed with all kinds of inside info, Jasmine scanned the internet to research Henderson-Cloy's history, their clients, their products, their stock, their financials. She had the luxury of an inside contact, and if she weren't successful in landing this job, with all this help, how could she ever succeed in landing a job with any other company?

Her dad quizzed her at night with the flashcards she'd made with facts about the company and information provided by Tessa. She reviewed her own fashion projects and photos over and over until she could see them clearly with her eyes closed. She thought about her own goals and motivations for her career and put them into words, practicing them over and over until they made sense.

"Finding a job is such hard work," she lamented to her dad.

"Yes, it is. But this one will be the hardest. Your first. Once you get your foot in the door and you gain experience, the next ones will be much easier."

Her dad insisted on her arriving in New York the day before the interview and he handed her his credit card to pay for her hotel room. "You don't want to be stressed out from driving into the city, and going straight to your interview. Drive up the day before, get your bearings, review your notes. You'll be much better prepared to put your best foot forward."

He was being such a gem, and he obviously wanted to help her succeed. "You might want to bring someone with you," he suggested. "Someone to help you navigate and find your way. Also, there's safety in numbers in the city."

That's when it hit her. "Do you mind if I invite Dax to come with me? He's in Ithaca, which is only a few hours away."

Dad turned his head, studied her for a moment. "That may not be a bad idea."

Jasmine's heart warmed. Of course, she was an adult and didn't need his permission to take Dax with her. On the other hand, she didn't want to disappoint him by taking her boyfriend. Although Dad had made an immoral decision in his own life, she hoped he trusted her to make moral decisions in hers.

She jumped up and gave him a kiss on the cheek. "Thanks, Daddy."

He patted her cheek with his hand. "You're going to knock it out of the park, sweetheart."

She called Dax and told him all the progress on preparing for her interview.

"You sound ready. Good for you."

"So, I have a question for you. Would you be willing to come to New York with me?"

"When?"

"Day after tomorrow. You take a train into the city and I'll meet you at Grand Central Station. We check into our hotel. Hang out, then spend the night. I go to my interview the next day."

"Yeah, sure."

"You can get off work?"

"Tomorrow I'll work on clearing my schedule."

Her heart jumped. "Great! I'll be so glad to have you there. And, just so you know, my dad thought it was a good idea for you to go with me."

"Your private bodyguard."

"Yes. I'm safe with you."

"Hmmmm."

"Dax, when you get to the central terminal, look for the Pegasus constellation. I'll be standing underneath it."

"The what?"

"Grand Central has a historic mural painted on its ceiling. Look up for the flying horse. That's our meeting point."

* * *

At eight o'clock at night, six days after she'd sent a Private Message to Fran Chambers, the Private Message notification dinged. Jasmine had progressively obsessed over it for days, worked to put it out of her mind, determinedly ignored it, and finally, forgot all about it. Until it dinged.

Then it all came flooding back.

She pulled out her phone and read the message. "Yes, I know the girl who gave up the baby in Pittsburgh nearly fifty years ago. She was one of my best friends from high school."

Jasmine waited for a second message. There had to be one. Someone wouldn't just write a cliffhanger like that and think that was the end of it.

Evidently, Fran would.

After a tortuous four-minute wait, Jasmine wrote, "I'd love to talk to you about this. Could I give you a call?"

Fran responded with a phone number. Jasmine punched it into her cell. The "hello" on the other end sounded a little brittle.

"Hi, Fran." Jasmine's heart was racing, resulting in a pounding in her ears that she hoped wouldn't impede her hearing. "This is Jasmine Malone."

"So you would be Crystal's granddaughter."

Jasmine gasped. This was happening. Her grandmother had a name. "Crystal? Crystal is her name?"

"Yes."

A million thoughts ran through her head, leaving bits of coherency behind. This was the answer to the mystery. Or, the woman was a fraud, feeding her incorrect information. Or, there were more than one Phone Booth Baby in Pittsburgh, and this was the wrong one.

Or, this was the answer to the mystery. How would she ever find out if she didn't settle down and talk to this woman?

"So, if you don't mind, tell me the story of Crystal and her baby."

"We were sixteen. We were in the musical at school together. Crystal and I both loved theater, and we were both going to graduate from high school and go to New York to become professional actresses. I mean, that was our dream. Anyway, we had tried out for the high school musical, and we were in rehearsals. Two weeks before opening night, Crystal couldn't hold back her tears onstage. The director forced her backstage and told her to get control of herself. I was worried about her, and followed her off. That's when she told me. She was pregnant."

Jasmine exclaimed, "Sixteen?"

"Yes. And we went to a conservative school in a time when that was frowned upon, to say the least. I asked her what she was going to do, and she had no idea. She didn't want to tell her parents, but she was going to have to. There was no choice but to have the baby, and she couldn't do it alone.

"She was far enough along that her costumes weren't going to fit. They could be altered, but it was about to become obvious. She'd hidden it for months. But she couldn't hide it any longer. Ultimately, she told her parents and although they were not happy, they let her drop out of school till after the baby was born. They told her from the beginning they would not allow her to keep the baby, and they would not raise her child. So Crystal had it in her mind that she'd have the baby, then give it up for adoption.

"By the time the baby was born, her emotions had gotten a little twisted. When she went into labor, she was home alone. The baby was born about four hours later in the bathtub. That little girl had that baby all by herself. She never even called her parents for help."

"How awful." Jasmine, at twenty two, couldn't imagine doing that. Let alone when she was sixteen.

"When her parents got home, Crystal's mother broke down in tears. She wanted to comfort Crystal and help her take care of the baby. But her dad didn't want to risk that the two women would get emotionally attached and want to keep her. He separated the women from the baby and took care of her himself, all night."

Jasmine brushed something from her cheek and was mildly surprised to see that tears covered them. She sniffed. This was her mother they were talking about – the baby in question. This poor, confused girl was her grandmother. Her heart was heavy and she felt just horrible for Crystal.

"When the morning arrived, Crystal woke up and snuck into her parents' room. She took the baby, wrapped her up and left before they even awoke. She walked to the bus stop and took the early bus into the city. She knew she couldn't keep the baby; she couldn't take care of her, and she didn't want to. But she didn't want her parents, her father particularly, to win on this one. Her parents had arranged to take the baby to the hospital and meet with the nuns and sign the baby over for adoption. But she wanted to take this matter into her own hands. It wasn't smart, and it wasn't right, but she did it her own way, not her parents' way.

"She got downtown and the baby woke up and started crying. She had no experience with babies, and had no idea what to do. She didn't know how to feed her, or even what babies ate. I mean, she knew nothing, the poor child! She thought if she got the baby to the hospital, they'd help her. They wouldn't let a baby die. But then it started raining. The baby, wrapped in a bath towel, was getting wet. Crystal looked around and saw a phone booth. She went in there and closed the door. It was shelter from the storm.

"In that phone booth, is the first time she'd actually held her daughter, comforted her, sang her a song, talked to her, got her to stop crying. It was the first time she'd acted like a mother. The first time she felt like a mother. She knew she wouldn't be a mother for long because she was too young, and didn't have the means to raise this beautiful little girl. But there was something special about this little place. It's where she and her daughter bonded."

Jasmine sobbed. She was crying openly.

"Oh sweetie, don't cry. It all turned out okay in the end, didn't it?"

Jasmine took a moment to pull herself together. "Yes."

"Your mother got adopted by a nice family, lived a good life?"

"Yes, she did. She's still happy and healthy and in love."

"Oh, that's good to hear."

"Fran, thank you so much for telling me this story. Don't take this the wrong way, but is it true? This isn't a hoax, is it? I mean I guess if it was a hoax, you wouldn't tell me, right?"

Fran chortled. "I know exactly why you're asking that. It's a deceptive world out there, and you don't know who you can trust. I know you don't know me from Adam, but I swear to you that I'm telling you the truth. The Pittsburgh papers caught wind of the story and put Crystal's baby in the spotlight for about a week. The Phone Booth Baby mystery. But I was the only one who knew, except of course for

Crystal and her parents. And they sure weren't going to say anything.

"Crystal begged me not to say a word, and of course, I didn't. It wasn't my story to tell, not back then. In fact, I've never told a single living soul that story until right now."

"Why me?" Jasmine asked, then regretted her bold question. She owed her gratitude to this woman. If Fran hadn't contacted her, she'd still be in the dark.

"I just got a feeling. I'm only on Facebook once a week, when I go to the library. I don't have internet where I live. Your post showed up on my Newsfeed and it was a blast from the past. I figured if it had broken the odds by reaching me, it must have been destined to reach me. I said a quick prayer to the Almighty and asked His guidance. I felt such an overwhelming sense of well-being, right away. That's when I sent you the note. I felt like God wanted me to reach out to you. Of course, I didn't see your response till my next weekly library visit. So here we are.

"You probably wonder if you can trust me. If you can believe this story. I want to assure you, you can."

Jasmine took a shaky breath. It was a nice sentiment, but even scammers tell their victims that they can trust them.

"Want to know why I say that, child?"

"Yeah. Why?"

"Because sometimes I go by another name, other than Fran Chambers. I go by Sister Mary Francis." Her words ended with laughter.

"You're a nun?" Jasmine exclaimed.

"Yes, I am."

Jasmine laughed.

"You can trust me."

They talked for several minutes about her nunship and her long career in the church. Retired now, she lived in a quiet little convent with other retired nuns, a very simple life, but one she treasured.

"So, whatever happened to Crystal?" Jasmine asked, her curiosity in this amazing story mounting. Her family history.

"She said a prayer over your mother, left her there in a basket and walked out. Never looked back. In fact, she went back to the bus station and took it straight to New York City."

"What? Why?"

"She never spoke to her parents again. The way they handled the pregnancy and the delivery made her cut ties with them. She was unable to get over it. That day, she started a new phase of her life. She was done with who she was before. She started her new life."

Jasmine sat and thought about all she had heard. "Oh, my gosh, Fran, my head's spinning with this revelation. It's going to take me a while to absorb all this. It's unbelievable. So, we know what happened after Crystal left her baby. Paul Mason came along, probably moments later, and found her, took her to the hospital. My grandparents adopted her a few days later. She had her happily ever after. A wonderful life."

Fran's voice softened. "I'm so glad to hear that. I'm thankful for this revelation as well. We both have a reason to thank our Creator today."

Jasmine nodded. "So what was Crystal's life like in New York?"

Fran cleared her throat. "We stayed in touch for a little while. I haven't actually talked to Crystal in decades. But she moved out there, finished high school, supported herself working odd jobs. Her love for the theater continued, and she was a very talented actress, so she managed to build up a resume in the theater. When I made my big life change and joined the convent, I lost touch with her."

"How old were you then?"

"Two days after high school graduation – I was eighteen."

"Wow." Jasmine imagined that was another story, but she was focused on this one first. This one that involved her own flesh and blood. Crystal was her mother's mother. Jasmine's grandmother. Then, "Is Crystal still alive?"

"I don't know for sure, dear. But I have no reason to believe she isn't."

"Is she still in New York, do you know?"

"I have no idea. But you could Google her, you know. I'm sure you'll come up with hits. I believe she's somewhat of a public figure."

Jasmine laughed. This retired nun in her sixties or seventies suggesting a Google search struck her as humorous.

"Crystal Blair. Good luck, dear. It's almost lights out for me. I need to go."

"Oh, Sister, thank you so, so much. I can't tell you how much this means to me. God bless you and thank you."

Chapter Sixteen

The secret was revealed. The story of Crystal Blair consumed her, kept her awake that night, and made adrenaline pump through her veins. She stayed up late that night to research her birth grandmother and as Sister Mary Francis suspected, there was a lot of material out there. Her entire career was chronicled in various articles and news features across the internet. Crystal Blair had made a mark on the New York theater scene.

Not necessarily as an actress. Yes, she had spent time on the stage, and doing her math, Jasmine calculated that Crystal had been a somewhat active actress from the time she was in her late teens, till her mid-twenties. At that point, she changed her focus to representing other actors. Over the next thirty years she became renowned for her very successful career as an agent to Broadway and off-Broadway stage actors. Scanning the list of clients, it was clear that she'd made a big difference for a lot of talented people.

The articles over more recent dates were scarce. Nothing indicated Crystal's death; however, she was probably retired or at the very least, slowed down. She did, however, still have an office address: Blair Talent Agency on Fifty Fourth Street. Jasmine wondered if she still went to work every day, or possibly stopped in to her namesake agency to check on the youngsters now running it.

After reading every article about her grandmother presented by the Google search, Jasmine clicked on Images. The screen popped up at least twenty pictures of Crystal Blair. She leaned closer to the screen and studied them.

They scanned at least forty years. A petite blonde, young Crystal was playing a role on stage, a profile view which made Jasmine catch her breath. Crystal could be Leslie's twin.

Another shot from the 1990's after she'd moved into her agency career. She stood behind a podium giving a speech. The resemblance to her mother was remarkable.

Jasmine opened a new window to pull up her Facebook account, and searched through for a picture of her mom. Finding a close-up shot, she dragged it and placed a picture of Crystal side by side.

If there had been any doubt that Sister Mary Francis had made up this story, it was confirmed now. Crystal Blair was Leslie's birth mother. Their physical similarities were uncanny.

The excitement in her heart popped to bursting level. This was big. This was exciting. And she'd be driving to New York tomorrow.

She would have to stop by Blair Talent Agency. She would just have to.

After a restless night's sleep, Jasmine called her mother. She wasn't sure how to tell her about her discoveries. Based on past conversations on the topic, she couldn't expect her to be excited about the news. But maybe Leslie would surprise her.

Sticking first to an update on her interview and travel plans, Leslie was thrilled and supportive, wishing her the best and knowing she would be successful.

Then, "Also, Mom, I have another item on my To Do list to accomplish while I'm up there." She launched into the story of the Facebook post that went viral, and the contact from Fran Chambers. When she started telling her Fran's connection to the teenaged mother of a baby in Pittsburgh, Leslie stopped her. "Jasmine. I don't like where this is going. Don't tell me you've been researching the story of my birth. Please don't tell me that, when I told you expressly that I didn't want you to."

Jasmine hesitated. "Mom, I …"

"Your job search is your priority right now. Getting your career started. That needs your full attention. Not some fifty year old newspaper clippings and your unhealthy fascination with them."

"I'm still doing my job search. Obviously. I have an interview in two days."

"But you are now distracted. This is a big break for you, Jas. Don't blow it because you're scatterbrained about this other thing."

This other thing? "Mom, you're acting like this is just an irrelevant little diversion. This is our family history. This is important, too."

"No. It's not our family history. Your grandparents are the ones who took me in when I was a few days old, and raised me as their very own. I have no interest or desire in knowing what happened with me before that. It doesn't matter."

"But I do …"

"But you shouldn't. Forget about it. Concentrate on your job search."

"She looks just like you."

The words hung out there, unanswered. Jasmine held her breath.

"What?" The syllable dripped with chill.

"I found her, Mom."

A brushing sound came over the line. Jasmine could picture her mom rubbing her hands over her eyes as she dealt with this new nugget of information. "Jasmine …," it was tired and resigned.

"I know the whole story about your mother, and her decision to abandon you, and what she did next. And I have a fairly good idea of where she is now."

"Jasmine, I can't. I just can't. This isn't right."

"Why? Aren't you in the slightest bit interested in hearing …?"

"No. My parents, Adele and Ken Somers of Pittsburgh, Pennsylvania, were two loving and generous and giving people who made me their own. It would be disrespectful to them to do this. They didn't care about the circumstances of my birth. They just loved me, unconditionally. I won't disrespect them by digging up history long buried. Where it belongs."

"Mommy," Jasmine murmured. She hardly ever called her that pet name anymore, but it held meaning to them both. A mother/daughter bond was a strong thing, but especially a mother/only child bond.

"Jas, I can't do this. I resent the fact that you threw this on me, against my wishes. I have enough going on in my life right now. This is the absolute last thing I need." Jasmine could tell she wanted to wrap up the phone call, pronto. "You have a safe drive, and call me when you get to New York. I wish you nothing but the best, honey, I do. But you've thrown me for a loop here, and I've got to think about this. Okay?"

"Okay, Mom. Listen, I didn't mean to hurt you. But this isn't just your family story. It's mine, too. This is my grandmother we're talking about."

"What about your Grandma Somers?"

"Yes! I love Grandma Somers. Tracking down your birth mother doesn't impact how I feel about Grandma Somers at all. Why does one have to impact the other?"

Leslie released a loud sigh. Then, a long pause. "I'm conflicted with this, honey. I feel like you betrayed me with this. I asked you to drop it and you went on, regardless. Now we have this ... person to deal with. Whether I want it or not. I need to pray about it."

* * *

Late the next afternoon, Jasmine stood in the center of Grand Central Station, and couldn't resist a Mary Tyler Moore moment. She dipped her head back, stretched her arms out and twirled in a circle. She smiled big and laughed out loud and figured that anyone looking would take note for twenty seconds or less, shrug their shoulders and move on. New York. It was an enigma.

She gazed up at the constellation mural painting on the vast ceiling. She remembered the Pegasus from a fifth grade fieldtrip. It had made an impression on her, and after the tour through the train station, she had come home and sought out the constellation in the night sky. She'd actually found it, or thought she had, and at any given chance, she and her mom would locate the flying horse made up of stars. Here in the station, she made her way to the wall and stepped around the perimeter, her head up, watching the mural.

She came to a stop under the horse and almost bumped into the solid chest of a male someone. "Excuse me," she said and darted her gaze straight into … Dax's startled gaze. He'd been walking with his head up, too. They burst into laughter and he pulled her into his arms. She breathed in deep and buried herself in his scent of soap and sunshine.

"Here we are," he said softly.

"Here we are." She'd always been one to rush ahead prematurely, and she'd always had to school herself to take one step at a time. To let things happen as they were supposed to happen. To be patient, and not to push.

But there was something about this moment, standing in each other's arms in New York City on the eve of an important job interview, which could lead to permanent employment and certainly a geographic move, with this man. This particular man, no other. "I'm glad you're here with me." Which was true, but boy, was it an understatement. She felt certain that it would have to be Dax, not anyone else. In her mind's eye she could picture their lives together falling into place. They move to New York, they both secure careers here, they get married, they ponder if the city is a place to raise a family.

"I'm glad I'm here, too."

She laughed out loud. Yep, way ahead of herself. They were here. She'd live in that moment and not get crazy. "Let's find our hotel."

They made their way, battling city traffic, directions and taxis. Close to two hours later, they received their keycard from their hotel clerk. "Enjoy your stay."

"Thanks," said Jasmine and stared at the single keycard. She glanced over at Dax. He had noticed too, and was looking at the card in her hand. "Umm, I just got one room."

He gave her an odd look, but she didn't know how to interpret it. It was sort of an eyebrow twitch, lopsided smile turned grimace. "Let's go find it."

They took the elevator to the fourteenth floor, following the number signs till they came to it. Dax took the card and opened the door. They pulled their luggage in and looked. It was small, as many New York hotel rooms were, but it was nicely appointed and had everything they needed. Including two double beds.

She sighed. "Can we not make the beds a weird thing?"

He smiled. "Of course. It doesn't have to be weird."

She held out a hand and he took it. She led him to the bed and they sat. "I have something to tell you. It's an embarrassing subject to talk about, but I'm thinking it's time. Dax, I'm …" she took a deep breath and blew it out, then pushed the words out in a huff, "I'm a virgin."

He nodded like it wasn't the most unexpected thing in the world. But he didn't say anything.

"I've always wanted to wait until my wedding night to have sex with my husband. It's important to me. But I gotta tell you, it wasn't easy to stay a virgin through college. My sorority sisters teased me, saying I was the World's Oldest Living Virgin. But it was just my thing, you know?"

He squeezed her hands and his lips curled into a small smile. "I understand."

"I want to be with you. But not like that. I'm not ready. You know?"

He nodded. Then he kissed her, a kiss that started soft and gentle but evolved to a breathtaking, heart racing joining of lips and tongues. She pulled back from him and studied his face. "So, this news is … okay with you?"

"Okay? Of course it's okay. It's great. It's fantastic."

She shook her head. She'd never encountered this reaction before. Not that she'd had this conversation a hundred times, but during the few relationships she'd had in college, she'd run into the need to explain. And in those cases, the guy's response was more an irritated rolling of the eyes, not a passionate kiss and the word fantastic. "Really? Why?" Then it dawned on her and she blurted it out before she considered better, "Are you a virgin, too?"

He laughed. "No, no I'm not. I made some mistakes – big ones – before I learned about Christ. By then, I'd already done some things that now, I'm no longer proud of. Some things that I can't undo – one of them was having sex with a woman who wasn't my wife. A woman I wasn't even in love with or committed to. But that's the thing with Jesus. He took all our sins and paid the ultimate price for them. No matter what I did before, He loves me and He forgives me. He paid the price for what I did wrong. Now, I want to live my life to honor Him. To glorify Him. It's not easy, and I still make mistakes every day. But He and I are going down the path together."

His thumb began rubbing her hand as he held her hands in both of his. "I'd been praying for God to lead me to the kind of woman I need. Someone who's already living the kind of life I aspire to. Someone to help guide me as a Christian, and yet someone I could fall in love with. That's when I met you. I believe God led you to me. This news? This is just confirmation that God has answered my prayer. Not only did he introduce us, not only are you a beautiful, sexy, talented woman. But you lead your life as God would have us live."

Her heart was pounding with the weight of his words. "Dax, I think you are giving me way too much credit. I am not perfect. Not by a long shot."

"Of course you're not! You're human. You make mistakes and God forgives you for those, too. But don't you see? You live a moral life. You're saving yourself for your wedding night, and that's exactly what God asks of us all. You're putting that into practice. I know it wasn't easy. But regardless, you're doing it. I support you in that."

A weight was starting to lift from her shoulders with the understanding of what he was saying. They would be partners in her celibacy. So many times she'd had to say no in the face of temptation, because of her decision to remain a virgin. So many times she'd had to watch a boyfriend walk away because she didn't provide him with the carnal pleasures that he felt came with the territory of a steady relationship. So many times she'd felt guilty for her decision, while knowing in her heart that she'd done the right thing.

So many nights she sat alone, wondering if there was a man out there for her, someone who was physically attractive to her, who she could build a future with, whose primary goal wasn't to change her mind – to convince her to give up her virtue before she was ready. And as her birthdays went by, with each passing year, she was convinced that unless she married straight out of college – like her mom did – there was very little chance that she'd find that man. Or, that she'd continue to consider her virginity a priority.

But Dax was the whole package. A gorgeous, sexy man she was physically attracted to, with the heart of a Christian and the beliefs to go along with it.

She threw herself into his arms and he pulled her close, stroking her hair. "I want to be intimate with you. I want us to kiss and hold and touch each other. I just don't want us to have intercourse. I don't want to have to reject you either. But I'm confused about how far to let it go until we stop."

He nodded. "I understand what you're saying. And I don't want that to be an issue in our relationship. So, you leave that to me, okay? I will never push the envelope with you. I will never push you beyond your limits."

"And you can ...?" She had no idea how to verbalize it since she never had to before. She huffed in frustration. She felt like such a naïve imbecile. "Um, I heard that guys get to a certain point in making out where they can't stop themselves, you know? It's physically impossible."

He shook his head. "That's bull. We can always stop. Don't believe it."

She gave him a shy smile, her heart pounding.

Her happiness was off the charts. She was so glad they'd had this difficult conversation. She said a silent prayer of thanks to God for bringing this man into her life.

"So," Dax said, drawing the syllable out, "we share a bed tonight and sleep in each other's arms?

She tilted her head back and smiled. "You bet."

Chapter Seventeen

After an hour spent testing out Dax's claim that taking passion to a certain limit, then putting the brakes on was a physical possibility, they left the hotel and hit the streets. They wandered around, taking note of their surroundings. Jasmine took out her phone, activated the GPS app and typed in the street address of her interview tomorrow. She had chosen the hotel because of its fairly close proximity to the interview, because she didn't want to rely on public transportation to get there. And once the car was parked in the hotel's parking garage, she didn't want to touch it again. If ... no, *when* she ended up moving to New York permanently, she'd already decided she wouldn't bring a car. She'd become a true New Yorker and learn the subways, the bus lines and become a pro at hailing cabs.

The interview was about five blocks away and they walked there and back easily. Because repetition would help her remember in the morning, they walked it one more time. Then they stepped into a tiny Italian restaurant next to the office of Henderson-Cloy and shared an antipasto salad and a pizza.

Back on the street, they blended into pedestrian traffic on the sidewalk and got the hang of aggressively stepping off the curb when the Walk light popped on, regardless of cars coming. They'd stop. Pedestrians had the right of way, and if they waited for all the cars to slide through, they'd never get across the street.

Jasmine plugged another address into her GPS and started following the directions.

"Where are you testing out now?"

Jasmine stepped out of the flow of foot traffic and pulled him out, too. They ducked into the doorway opening of a skyscraper on their block. "This one is just my curiosity. I found out my birth grandmother's name and business address."

Dax's mouth opened and he stared, silent. "You did?"

"Yes, and I know you said I should leave well enough alone. And I already know my mother does not approve of this research I've done. But I'm this close and I just have to at least check it out, you know?"

He leaned against the wall and gestured his hands to her. "Tell me."

She went through the entire course of events, starting with the phone conversation with Fran, and ending with the Google research she'd done. She pulled up Google Images on her phone and showed him a close-up of Crystal.

He stared, his eyes widening. He reached a hand up and ran it down his face. "My gosh."

"She's a carbon copy of my mom, right?"

He nodded. "Alarmingly so. Wow." She watched the wheels turn in his head. "So, your mother doesn't want you to find her. This woman – has she given you any indication that she wanted to be found? Do you have any idea how she would react if you confronted her?"

"Well, confront is a strong word. I mean, I wouldn't go storming in there and demand an explanation from my birth grandmother. But, to answer your question, no. She's shown no sign of trying to locate the daughter she gave up. She's built her own life here in New York. She's in the theater business. She was an actress, then an agent. She's represented lots of big name Broadway performers over the years. She's somewhat of a legend." She let her gaze drift back to the petite blonde beauty on her phone. "Although one interesting thing is that I don't believe she ever got married, and it doesn't appear that she ever had any children."

He met eyes with her and raised his eyebrows.

"Maybe she was so affected by giving up my mother that she couldn't go through it again."

He shrugged. "Or maybe she never wanted kids to begin with. Maybe she never fell in love. You don't know."

"True. But isn't that an even better reason to meet her? To talk with her and ask her these questions?"

He shook his head, a fierce shake. "No. I could see maybe writing her a letter. Maybe. Send it snail mail so she could ignore it if she wanted to. But nothing as demanding as an email, a phone call, or God forbid, a face-to-face visit. I just have a feeling that she wouldn't want that."

"Okay. But it couldn't hurt to just wander by her office, could it? She's probably not in there anyway. I imagine she's at least partially retired, if not fully."

He dipped his head, his chin hitting his chest but his eyes keeping contact with hers. An unspoken challenge.

"Dax, I'm this close. I'd regret it if I didn't go. Are you going with me? Because if not, I'm going anyway."

His mouth screwed into a frustrated frown. "Hardheaded women."

They followed the directions coming from the phone. Blair Talent Agency was located eight blocks north and two blocks west of Henderson-Cloy. After a moderate walk, they arrived. It was housed in a nondescript sky scraper, but once inside the front door, a brass plate, about a foot square, engraved with "Blair Talent Agency" was attached to the marble wall. The offices were located on the seventh floor.

Jasmine looked over at Dax, and he shrugged and walked to the elevator. As they rode up, he asked, "So, what's your plan?"

She thought for a second. "I won't introduce myself today, even if she's here. I'm in New York first and foremost for my job interview. I can't get distracted from that. We'll go to her office, check it out, and leave. Maybe before I leave tomorrow, I'll come back. Maybe."

He nodded and stepped off the elevator when the door slid open. They walked to the Blair door and peeked through the glass. On the other side was a small reception area. No one sat inside. Jasmine pulled the door open.

The walls of the waiting room were filled with framed photos of beautiful women and handsome men, smiling for the camera. In some of them, the good-looking people stood beside Crystal Blair. Jasmine studied the ones featuring her grandmother. A beautiful woman, Crystal rarely smiled. Even in the pictures where the others sported jubilant grins, her grandmother was refined and calm. Never frowning, but never one to appear particularly happy. Although Crystal and Leslie shared their looks, they did not share that particular trait. Her mom's joyfulness was one of Jasmine's favorite things about her.

Dax observed the pictures too, and when she'd completed a round, a receptionist came and sat behind a desk. "May I help you?"

Jasmine looked up, alarmed. She'd been so absorbed in her study, she hadn't noticed her arrival. "No, thank you. I'm fine."

The receptionist gave her a look of confusion. "Do you have an appointment with one of the agents?"

Jasmine shook her head.

"Are you an actress?"

Jasmine shook her head again.

"I'm sorry, ma'am, but this is a private office. You need to either make an appointment or you need to leave."

Dax took Jasmine's arm and turned her. "Our mistake. We're in the wrong suite."

The receptionist looked back to the work on her desk as they made their way to the door. Without warning, Jasmine turned back. "Is Crystal Blair expected in today or tomorrow?"

The receptionist looked back up. "Who's asking?"

That threw Jasmine. With no forethought to the story, she said, "I know I said I wasn't an actress, but I am. I was wondering if Crystal Blair would represent me."

The receptionist frowned. "None of our agents will see you without a personal invitation. And Crystal is no longer taking on new clients. Good day."

Dax tugged on her arm and pulled her out the door. A few steps away, he whispered harshly, "What was that all about?"

"I don't know! I panicked! We should've had a story lined up."

"If you'd stuck to the plan, we wouldn't have needed a story. You changed things mid-stream, and you drowned."

"I know. I'm terrible at espionage!"

They walked back toward the hotel, hand in hand. Eventually, Jasmine's pulse slowed to normal and she was able to enjoy the sights and sounds of the city around them. "I love the energy of this place. Everyone walking here and there, everyone with their own place to go, busy busy. You know, for such a big city with so many buildings and businesses, Manhattan doesn't cover that much ground. I looked it up before we came. One point six million people live here in roughly thirty-three square miles. Of course, that doesn't even count people like us, walking the streets, who don't live here."

Dax let his head drop back as they strolled, and he looked to the top of the skyscrapers. "That's amazing. Not my thing, necessarily. But it might be fun to live in this environment for a few years. Completely opposite from our last trip. Compare the lazy, peaceful lifestyle of Pawleys Island with this place."

Jasmine smiled. "Best of both worlds."

* * *

Evening slipped by and they headed to their room. Dax turned on the TV and put his feet up while Jasmine slipped into the bathroom. He got absorbed in a news magazine program of a rich housewife in Texas murdered in her home. It was going to be the husband. It was always the husband.

"Dax."

Her voice floated to him softly on the air. He looked up and his heart jumped into his throat. Jasmine. His Jasmine. Her hair hung in waves around her shoulders, shining like she had given it a brushing. Her skin gleamed and her lips were painted with a darker shade of pink. He stood and went to her, brought his hand up and rubbed his knuckles as gently as he could over her cheek. "You are so gorgeous, Jasmine."

She gave him a pleased smile and he leaned in and captured her lips. Pulling her body against him, he held her tight and concentrated on the joining of their mouths, the flip and flow of his tongue with hers. His hands wandered into her hair, and he ran his fingers through the strands. He tugged on her hair, pulling her head back slightly so he could angle in on the kiss.

She gasped and giggled. He pulled back and looked at her face, her eyes. "Jasmine."

"Dax." Her smile emerged and he felt the flush caused by his racing pulse color his face.

The time felt right, although he couldn't be sure. His admission could have the result of calling their amorous activity to a sudden halt. But he'd been feeling it and he could no more keep it unspoken, than he would refuse to take his next breath.

He held her face in both hands and lifted so she was looking straight in his eyes. "Jasmine, I love you."

She gasped and her eyes blinked wildly, a tear visible in the corner.

Plunging forward, he continued, "I am in love with you. You're beautiful and talented and smart and loving. You are a woman of God and you are the answer to my prayers. You and I could build our lives together. Be together and walk through our lives together, loving each other."

He was just rambling now, but he couldn't help it. The woman filled him with an uncontrollable need to tell her his feelings, to put into words the unspeakable language of emotions. He was in completely untraveled territory. He'd never told a woman he loved her before, and he'd never felt this strong a feeling for anyone. But despite that, he knew it. He recognized it. This was that emotion that so many songs had been written about, that so many movies tried to replicate. This was the real deal.

Now, he just needed to hear a similar sentiment from her. Because he'd be brokenhearted if she didn't return his love.

And in her next breath, he got it. "I love you too. I do. I can't stop thinking about you when we're apart. I can't wait to see you again. I can't wait to hold your hand and touch your face. I love it when you're next to me. With you beside me, I can do anything. We are a team, you and I. I love the idea of traveling through our lives together. And you get my desire to stay pure until my wedding day. That's huge, Dax. You can't know how important that is. We're in synch. Our backgrounds are as opposite as they come. But today, we are a perfect match."

She stood, her chest heaving with breathlessness. His gaze roamed over her face. Then he lifted her up and carried her to the bed and placed her on top of it.

She blinked at the sudden distance between them while he stood beside the bed. She reached out a hand, and that was all the invitation he needed. He climbed onto the bed, over her and lowered himself beside her. He wrapped his arms around her and breathed her in. She rested a hand on his abdomen and ran her fingers over the ridge of his muscles. He caught her gasp.

They explored each other, the curves and lines of the other's body. There was time, he reminded himself. They had endless time in their future. Keeping his mind in tune with his promise to her, balanced with his need to discover her, the hours passed.

Chapter Eighteen

Jasmine stared into the heavily lit mirror in the hotel bathroom, putting the final touches on her eyelashes and lips. She wasn't a big makeup user on a regular basis – just a smear of liquid foundation and a brush of powder generally did it. She was taking extra care this morning because, well, she was in New York and she was about to interview for her dream job in fashion. It just seemed the thing to do.

Throw in the added benefit that she and Dax were now officially in love, and the morning couldn't get any better.

He came in behind her, looked at her reflection in the mirror and said in a low, deep voice that made her stomach feel funny, "Gorgeous."

She pushed him away. It was hard enough to concentrate on her interview knowing he was in the next room, warm and rumpled from their night together. Transplant the man directly behind her, his long hair still mussed from the pillow, wearing the shorts he'd determinedly kept on all night for her, along with his bare yummy chest, and there's no way she would get out the door.

He chuckled, left the bathroom and turned on the TV in the room.

Jasmine sighed happily and picked up her hairbrush. Last night was one of a kind. It was passionate, it was intimate, it was loving. And yet, their amorous activity had never once crossed the line into the inappropriate. They both were committed, together, to a chaste, pure romance. And that took such a load of worry off her mind. No need for her to be the make out police, always being the one to say no and put a damper on a romantic evening. They were on track with the same goals.

Knowing that lifted all kinds of restrictions. With Dax's promise that he wouldn't put her in a position of no return, their intimacy could be enjoyed and savored.

This was not only new to her, it was new to Dax as well. There were times last night when she knew Dax had to physically remove himself from her to regain control, but he always returned, kissed her and put the brakes on.

She was so in love.

Turning out the light, she headed back to the room and did a runway flip for him. "Do I look all right?"

She could count on him to give her a compliment, but what she meant was, did she look like a New York fashion designer? Or did she look like a small town girl pretending to be one? The distance between the two was vast, and could make the difference between landing the job or not.

He rose to his feet, took her by the shoulders and landed a kiss on her forehead. "You look like you already work here."

Perfect. That's what she needed to hear.

He looked at the clock on the TV. "You've got over an hour. Want to grab some breakfast?"

She picked up her leather shoulder bag containing her resume and her portfolio photos, and hugged it against her side. "Too nervous to eat."

His eyebrows darted up. "Get something inside you. Some fruit or a muffin or something. You might get dizzy with an empty stomach."

She laughed. He sounded just like her mom.

She perked her lips and they shared a quick kiss. "I'll grab something at a street vendor. I think I'll walk leisurely and make sure I have plenty of time."

He nodded and squeezed her shoulders, then let her go. "Knock 'em dead, sweetheart. I know you can do it." She smiled brightly at him. In unison, they said, "I love you."

They laughed together and Dax said, "I'm going to like saying that to you any chance I can."

"Keep it coming. Bye."

Jasmine made her way down to the hotel lobby, then out onto the street. She pulled up her phone GPS and set the verbal directions on the last destination on Fifty Fourth Street. Foot traffic was much heavier this morning than yesterday afternoon when they were out and about, so it took her longer to reach her destination.

"You have arrived at your destination," said the GPS and Jasmine looked around, confused. This wasn't Henderson-Cloy. This was ... oh shoot! This was Blair Talent Agency. She'd told the GPS the wrong address!

Her first impulse was to panic. She'd sabotaged her own success today. Now she'd be late to her interview, which was never acceptable. But then she took a breath and calmed herself. She had plenty of time. She glanced at her phone. Although she'd have to book, she had purposely left lots of time to arrive at her interview and review her materials. She was fine. She would be fine.

She glanced over at the building and ducked inside for a quiet refuge. Standing inside the lobby, she pushed buttons on her GPS app, now pulling up the proper street address. Two pretty young women walked by on their way to the elevator. A snippet of their conversation floated to her, "So excited to see Crystal today. She must've scheduled this for the one day a week she comes in. She said she had something for me..." and then they stepped onto the elevator.

Jasmine turned, watching their movement, shaking her head when they'd disappeared. Crystal was coming in today. It had to be Crystal Blair. Who else would they be talking about? Curiosity overcoming her, she jumped onto the next elevator. Riding it up to the seventh floor, she walked to the office door. She peeked in and saw the two women from the elevator sitting in the waiting area, as well as several other attractive people, actor types, she assumed. It was a busy morning at Blair Talent. Probably because Crystal was making her weekly appearance.

She debated going in and sitting down, but decided against it. What point would it serve? The nasty receptionist would most likely remember her and kick her out for loitering. She still wasn't sold on revealing her identity to Crystal – she hadn't put nearly enough thought into that yet, and with her mother's admonishment that it wasn't her mystery to solve – she wanted to honor her wishes, and stay incognito. Yet, she had an undeniable need to at least be close to the woman who shared her DNA. Listen to her voice. See her in person. Observe her interacting and make a decision about the kind of person she was. Successful, yes. She'd accomplished a lot in her lifetime. But what about her manner? The way she was with people. Was she kind? Was she horrible? These were the questions she hoped to answer while in New York.

Time passed quickly as her mind wandered. Her imagination pulled up an extremely believable, but entirely pretend relationship between her and Crystal, one where they walked the streets of Manhattan together, attended Broadway premieres, ate at Sardi's and wore high heeled shoes. She had no idea how long she stood there, how many minutes were eaten up with her thoughts. But when she glanced at the time, it gave her a jolt. She was late. The GPS was telling her the walk would take eighteen minutes, and now, her interview was a mere ten minutes away.

She'd never make it.

Alarmed and furious with herself for creating this unneeded crisis, she ran for the elevator. Dialing Dax, she barely waited for him to answer before she exclaimed, "Dax, I'm late! I came to the wrong address and now I don't have time to get back to my interview." The elevator door opened and she raced into the lobby, then out onto the street. "I'm so stupid! Why did I do this? The interview's in ten minutes!"

Dax's voice emerged like a calm in the storm. "You're going to be fine. Take a deep breath and relax. You don't have time to walk. You need to hail a cab. Walk to the curb." She did. "Make sure the flow of the traffic is going the direction you need. In other words, you may have to cross the street to go in the right direction."

Jasmine shrugged but saw a taxi approaching.

"Hold your hand up and yell. If they see you, and they have an open cab, they'll stop for you."

His words seemed to narrate the reality in front of her. She raised her hand at the cab driver, they met eyes and the cab pulled up beside the curb directly in front of her. "Thank you, Dax. I got one," she said breathlessly. She accidently hung up on his well wishes, but he'd understand.

She stepped carefully off the curb into the street. Last thing she needed now was a twisted ankle. She reached for the door handle but it swept open on its own accord. She gasped and pulled back. Someone was emerging from the cab onto the street.

A very familiar someone. A petite, blonde someone Jasmine had seen in a hundred photos over the last week. Only this time, she wasn't her pretend grandmother conjured in her fantasies. It was her grandmother in the flesh: Crystal Blair.

Crystal startled, looked up at Jasmine. Jasmine held the taxi's door open for her and stepped aside. Then words came out without plan, "Crystal Blair."

The older woman stood, brushed her skirt and said, "Yes. Hello." She walked on by and Jasmine turned and watched her pull open the door and enter the building.

Her first real-life connection to her past.

She shook it off, and climbed into the cab. Now, it was time to make connection with her future.

* * *

She arrived four and a half minutes after her scheduled interview time. She paid the cabbie, climbed out and raced to the front door. Then she drew a deep breath, closed her eyes and prayed. *Lord, be with me. Your will be done. You know what You're doing, so if You want me here, then bless me as I go into this interview. Send Your words through me. Let me be Your vessel. Send me the confidence to impress them and let me show them what I can do.*

She squared her shoulders, lifted her chin and walked into the building. She wasn't sure if it was God's peace that enveloped her, or if she'd established it herself, but all sign of her previous panic was gone. It didn't matter. God had her back, and she had this.

Riding the elevator, she ran through her message points in her mind. She arrived in the waiting room and gave her name to the receptionist. The woman nodded, held up a finger, then pointed to a chair. Jasmine sat, held her portfolio, and concentrated on being calm.

"Jasmine Malone." A woman in a dress and jacket had said her name. Of course she was put together perfectly.

"That's me." Jasmine stood and joined her, holding out her hand.

"Hello, Jasmine. I'm Caitlyn Morris. I'll be interviewing you, along with John Henderson."

Jasmine recognized the names from the research she'd done and the quizzing her dad had helped drill into her head. "So nice to meet you."

Ms. Morris led her down a short hallway to an office, and through the door. A man was seated at a table, and Ms. Morris stepped to sit beside him, gesturing to Jasmine to sit facing them. She sat gracefully, crossed her legs at the ankle and rested her portfolio on the floor. She looked up at them expectantly, a calm smile on her face.

"Thanks for coming. You come highly recommended."

"I'm thrilled to be here. And I appreciate Tessa's recommendation. Her endorsement of my skills in fashion design is flattering."

Ms. Morris and Mr. Henderson dived into a series of questions. Jasmine wasn't sure if they'd intended it or not, but they came across as Good Cop/Bad Cop. However, the roles kept changing. Sometimes she was friendly, he was rough, then they switched roles. They asked a variety of questions that required her to extract knowledge from her internship last summer, or from her college classwork. She didn't need to wonder if she'd gotten a relevant Fashion

Merchandising education at Cornell, because judging from the variety of questions they asked, she had.

Then they pulled out paper printouts of her photos and grilled her about different photography choices she'd made, how she'd positioned the models, and why she'd designed the clothes the way she'd chosen to. Jasmine kept up, at least she thought she had. She wanted this job very much. She hoped she was presenting that desire. But if they didn't hire her, she hoped she could accept that decision and not blame herself for poor performance.

Finally, the questions filtered to a stop. Ms. Morris and Mr. Henderson looked at each other and nodded. "One more question. Why do you want this job? Why Henderson-Cloy?"

Jasmine took a breath. "I'd be honored to start my career at Henderson-Cloy. You have a reputation for quality and a diverse offering of fashions. Your designers are top in their field, and I would be thrilled to apprentice under any of them. This is exactly what I want. I want to live in New York and build my career in the field that I've trained in. I just need a chance to show you what I can do. And I promise I will work hard."

A smile popped out and covered Ms. Morris' face. She tapped on the stack of photos. "We were impressed by your portfolio." She gazed over at her partner, then back at Jasmine. "I think I can speak for Mr. Henderson when I say we could use someone with your energy and talent. Give us a week to convene and prioritize our candidates." She stood and held her hand out to Jasmine. They shook. "Best of luck to you."

* * *

Dax sat in silence in the hotel room. He'd run through his thoughts in his mind over and over during the last two hours. He'd come to a decision, and prayed about it. He knew what he had to say, and he had to let the consequences fall as they may. Even if the worst happened, and he lost Jasmine for good.

She entered the room and tossed her purse on the bed, stepping out of her heeled shoes. Her beauty reached out and grabbed him and his body reacted in a way that made him remember their night of chaste passion. But he couldn't let their night together impact what he felt was right.

"Hi," he said and she jumped. Her face beamed with happiness at the sight of him.

"Hi," she breathed and rushed over to him. He rose to his feet and she took his cheeks in her hands and moved in for a kiss. He closed his eyes and absorbed her. She pulled back. "I did it."

"You got the job?"

"Well, no," she laughed. "I got through the interview. First things first."

He smiled and they sat together on the couch. "Congratulations. How did it go?"

She gave him an animated summary of the questions and her answers, and her impressions of the interviewers and the office. They had even taken her on a tour of the offices and the warehouse. She was enamored with the place. He hoped and prayed she would get this opportunity. She seemed to have done well, at least from his perspective. Of course, what did he know about fashion? But he wanted her to get her heart's desire, and this certainly seemed to be it.

When her words ran out, she rested happily into the couch and held his hand. It killed him to have to bring up an unpopular topic, but he knew he must. "Jasmine, there's something I need to say to you."

She looked up through her eyelashes at him.

"You're way out of control on this Crystal Blair thing."

She took in a breath and pushed it out. "I know. I …"

"No, let me." He twisted in his seat to face her. "You said you wouldn't let it distract you from your job search, but that's exactly what you did. You were late to your interview, and you had to pull yourself back together so you could interview properly."

"I prayed to God for strength in my interview."

"Well, it's good you called on Him for help, but you never should've put yourself in this position. You are single-mindedly obsessed on this woman, and it's unhealthy. You need to let it go."

She studied him for a moment. "Or what?"

"Or you'll never realize the abundance of life that God has planned for you."

She frowned, thinking. "Why?"

"Because this isn't what He wants for you. This isn't your battle to fight. This isn't your treasure to unearth. This is for your mother to decide. You're trying to have your cake and eat it too."

She looked down at her lap. "I'm being selfish."

"Yes. At the risk of hurting your mother and her mother. Let it go, baby."

"It's hard for me to let things go."

He let out a laugh. "Yeah, I get that. At first I thought you were greedy. You're so used to things going your way, that you want everything. But what you said about that verse in Matthew made sense to me. God wants us to live in abundance, and we need to have faith enough to reach for it."

She nodded. "But not this."

"Not this. Give this back to your mother and let her decide what to do with it."

Chapter Nineteen
(Two weeks later …)

Jasmine couldn't help but let out a squeal as they drove across the bridge that led from Myrtle Beach to Pawleys Island. Dax reached over from the driver's seat and squeezed her hand, then raised them both through the open sunroof of the car. Maybe she'd start a savings account for a convertible. How awesome would it be to make her entrance to Pawleys with her and her handsome boyfriend's hair blowing in the wind.

They maneuvered the familiar route to The Old Gray Barn. Hank and Leslie were expecting them, but they had no inkling of the good news Jasmine had to share.

Dax pulled the car underneath the house on stilts and before they could get fully out, Hank and Leslie emerged from the house. Everyone exchanged hugs, handshakes and happy greetings.

They went to the sunporch facing the ocean, everyone settling into Adirondack rockers. Leslie brought out a tray with a pitcher of iced lemonade and glasses.

"Oh, Mom! Before we drink that – I have something else we can share."

Leslie looked over at her, mid-pour. "Huh?"

"Hold on just a second!" She winked at Dax, jumped up and dashed out. In her suitcase, she found the carefully wrapped bottle of bubbly she'd bought expressly to make her announcement, along with four plastic champagne glasses. She carried them back to the porch.

"Dax, will you do the honors?" She handed him the bottle and he started work on removing the cork.

"Jasmine," Leslie said slowly. "What are you …?"

A loud pop made them all jump and Jasmine quickly filled the glasses, handed them out. "We have reason to celebrate. I nailed my interview! Henderson-Cloy just made me a job offer!"

A wall of congratulatory sound arose and both Leslie and Hank pulled Jasmine into a hug. "Couldn't be happier for you, darlin'," said her stepfather. The look on her mom's face broadcasted her happiness without any words necessary.

They settled down in their rockers, and talked excitedly. Although the offer was new, Jasmine had made several preliminary plans. The start date was three weeks away. She'd enjoy her last visit to Pawleys. She and Leslie would head back to New York to hunt for an apartment. She'd be ready to start work when they wanted her.

"We spent most of the interview talking about my photos and models. In fact, if Dax, Emma or Stella ever wanted to do some freelance modeling work, Henderson-Cloy would be interested in signing them!"

"We'll have to tell the girls," Leslie said with a smile.

"They were very nice to me. Very welcoming. That friend of Roxanne's – you know, Marianne's actress – Roxanne's friend Tessa works for Henderson-Cloy and she put in a good word for me. In fact, I believe it was the personal endorsement that made the difference for me. They knew they wanted me from my photos. I get the impression from Tessa that the job was mine to lose."

Dax turned his head and gave her a meaningful expression. She ignored him, but unfortunately her eagle-eye mother notice.

"What?"

Jasmine sighed. "I guess it's safe to tell you now, since I did get the offer. But I almost blew it. The morning of the interview, I ended up going over to your mother's office."

She paused, knowing this choice of words would irritate her mother. She wasn't disappointed. "Jasmine, I wish you would just drop this craziness! How many times do I have to tell you, …?"

Jasmine laughed and raised her voice to interrupt her mom's rampage. "I was that close, Mom, and I just wanted to see her. And I did."

That shut her up. "You actually saw her?"

"Yes, and I spoke to her. Well, sort of. I said her name."

Leslie's mouth opened.

"But I came to my senses. I wasn't about to let my fixation on the past ruin my chances for a good future. So I left her there on the streets of New York, jumped in the cab, and raced off to my interview."

Leslie was still speechless, but at least she nodded. Jasmine turned toward her and took her hands in her own. "Mom, I've decided not to contact … your birth mother. I'm going to leave that to you to decide. It's your past, not mine. But I did all the legwork for you. I know her name, I know her career, her history, her work address and phone number. And I wrote it all down for you."

She dropped her mom's hands and picked up the big manila envelope she'd brought in and rested on the table. She handed the sealed envelope to her mom. "It's all there. You decide. Meanwhile, I'm done." She stepped closer to Dax and sat on his knee. "Because a wise man once told me, what's past is past. Your past does not define your future. All things are new in Christ Jesus."

She looked down at him and he was smiling at her. She kissed him.

Leslie fingered the thick envelope. She ran her finger over the sealing and then dropped it into her lap. "I think the right thing to do would be to talk to my mom about it. My real mom. The mom who loved me and raised me and made me her own. See if she wants to review these papers together. If she's comfortable with it, then I probably will be, too."

* * *

Later, Leslie led Jasmine into her bedroom to take a look at some new clothes. Dax and Hank were alone on the sunporch. Dax looked over at him. Hank was the kind of man who loved his family. It was that simple. He worked hard all day with the goal of providing for the ones he loved. He was the kind of man Dax would be lucky to grow closer to.

"Hank?"

"Hmmm?" Hank looked over at him and smiled casually.

"I have something I want to talk to you about."

Hank cleared his throat and moved his rocker so he could see Dax a little better. "Sure thing. Shoot."

He'd practiced it at least a dozen times in his head. He'd even silently run through it several times in the car with Jasmine right beside him. Now was the time to pull those rehearsed words out. And shoot if he couldn't remember them.

"Um." He looked up at Hank's eyes, and they crinkled as they relaxed into a calm smile.

"Tongue tied? I think I might know what this is about."

Dax shook his head. He couldn't possibly know.

"You're wondering what will happen to you and Jasmine, now that she's starting her career in the big city?"

Well, the man was heading in the right direction, but not exactly. "You're halfway right. Jasmine's moving to the big city, true. But I want to end up there, too. Eventually. Not quite yet." Well, shoot. This wasn't going well. "I'm sorry. Hold on." He dug in the pocket of his khaki shorts and pulled out a small velvet box. He flipped it open and showed it to Hank. A small but clear diamond sparkled from its resting spot in the box.

And Dax decided right then and there that he'd love Hank forever because he got a big, happy smile on his face. And if he looked that happy, then Dax had to bet he'd be supportive. He grappled his courage and went on. "Hank, I love your daughter. Well, your stepdaughter." He flashed him a smile. "She's a phenomenal woman. She's smart and brave and ambitious. I've learned so much from her that I wouldn't know if I hadn't met her. She's got a strong faith in God, and I want to be a faithful follower. I think we have a great future ahead of us, and I want to ask for your approval to propose to her tonight."

Hank rose, held a hand out for Dax, then pulled him to his feet and into a strong embrace. He patted Dax's back and when he ended the hug, he had to wipe a few tears from his eyes with his knuckles. "Young man, I couldn't be happier for you. I give you my approval wholeheartedly. Not that you need it."

Dax smiled and shook his hand. "Thank you."

"Ahh, but wait. You're not quite there yet, youngster. You know there are two more parents you need to talk to if you want to get approval from all of us. One of them's here in this house, but the other one's about seven hours away."

Dax nodded. "I figured I'd start with you. If I needed to adjust my approach, you could give me pointers."

Hank laughed. "Nope, put that one on tape and play it back. It was perfect."

Leslie and Jasmine returned at that moment. Dax scurried to get the box back in his pocket. Hank looked over at Dax, winked at him and stepped over to Jasmine. "Hey, can I convince my favorite stepdaughter to take a walk with me on the beach?"

Jasmine wrapped her arm through his. "Of course!"

Leslie turned and headed for the door. "A walk is a great idea, sweetie." She was using her big toe to flip off her sandals when Hank looked over her head and gave Dax an exaggerated eyebrow gesture.

"Actually!" Dax blurted, and both Jasmine and Leslie looked over at him, alarmed. "Leslie, could I get some advice from you? In the kitchen."

Jasmine frowned but Leslie went along with him without question.

* * *

Late that night, Hank and Leslie had retired and Dax and Jasmine were relaxing in front of the TV in the great room. It had been a happy family day, everyone congratulating her on her new job. Her heart swarmed with excitement for the upcoming adventure. She would be living in New York, working in the fashion industry, designing fashions for

Broadway clients. One perk of the job was free tickets to the plays they outfitted. She couldn't wait. And the fact that Dax would only be a few-hour drive away, instead of a seven-hour drive away, was icing on the cake.

She stretched the kinked muscles out of her spine and glanced over at Dax. He was messing with his phone. "What are you doing?"

He looked up at her and stuffed the phone in his pocket. "Nothing."

She shrugged and picked up the remote control. "Anything you interested in watching?"

"No." He stood. "In fact, let's go out. Let's stretch our legs and listen to the ocean waves."

"Sure." She grinned. She adored the fact that in two short visits, he'd fallen in love with the beach just as deeply as she had over her entire life. Just another thing to love about the man.

They walked to the sunporch, then out the back door. Down the stairs and onto the sand. "Oooh, the sand gets so cold after the sun goes down."

He stepped closer and put an arm around her. "I'll keep you warm," he said with a laugh. Then, "Do you want to go get a sweatshirt?"

"Nah, I'm fine."

They headed toward the water's edge, then walked to their left, letting the waves run over their toes and up to their ankles. His arm around her kept the chill of the air away, and she wrapped hers around his waist.

A little distance down, he said, "Okay, let's stop here." She faced him and they made a little isolated circle from the wind consisting of just themselves. "I love you, Jasmine."

"I love you, too. And I love being able to tell you I love you, because I know you love me, too." They laughed and shared a warm kiss.

Dax pulled her a little tighter. "Jasmine, you are the woman I have been looking for my entire life. I believe that you and I were placed here in this time, and this place, specifically for each other. I like to picture God looking down from heaven, smiling because we've found each other."

Jasmine smiled. "I love that image."

"Before I met you I was fearful about love. I was always afraid that I wasn't good enough, that even if I was lucky enough to find a good woman, that I wouldn't live up to her level. You helped me get past that. You and I come from about as different pasts as two people can. But being with you has made me a better man. You've made me more confident in myself, in my abilities, in my future."

She touched his cheek. "You've made me a better woman, Dax. I always just breezed through life, never really thinking about consequences. I always tried to be a good person, but I never really scratched too far beneath the surface. You've helped me grow up. You've helped me see what kind of person I should strive to be. You've helped me grow a stronger faith. You've helped me pull God more into my daily decisions and life."

"Where I'm weak, you're strong," he said.

"And vice versa."

"So, being confident in the couple that we are, and the love that we have, I have taken a step toward our future. Our future, Jasmine, you and me."

Jasmine froze, her eyes flying to his. But it was so dark out here on the beach that she could barely make out the lovely cocoa-brown eyes that she loved so much. He must've read her mind because he held up a finger, said, "Just a moment," and pulled his phone out again. With one swipe he activated some soft music from his iTunes library. And with another swipe, he turned on his flashlight. His beautiful face was bathed in a bright light while Billy Joel sang *Just the Way You Are*. He handed her the phone. "Could you hold this?"

She did, and he pulled one thing more out of his pocket, something dark, which he kept wrapped in his hand. Then he lowered himself to the sand, resting on one knee.

Her intake of breath was involuntary.

"Jasmine, I can't imagine my life without you in it. I want to devote myself to you, and you to devote yourself to me, as man and wife. In hopes that you'll say yes, I picked this out for you." He opened his palm, popped open a velvet box of midnight blue. She shone the flashlight on it and a diamond on a plain gold band reflected back at her. "Will you marry me?"

She screamed and fell down on her knees too, grabbed his jaw and pulled him in for a long kiss. "Yes! Yes yes yes. I will marry you, Dax, with pleasure." She extended her left ring finger to him.

He laughed and fumbled the ring out of the box. He held it tightly in his hand, then slid it gracefully onto her finger. "We don't have to rush." He stared into her eyes. "I just want you to know how I feel about you, and about our future together."

They sat back on the sand and held each other. Billy Joel wrapped up his love song and Dax snapped it off. "I got permission from all three of your parents," he said.

"You're kidding! Oh, my gosh. Over and above the call of duty."

"They all approved."

"Well, of course they did. You're the best guy I've ever known."

They rose, wiped sand off their legs and headed back to The Old Gray Barn, their future of possibilities as vast as the sky above them.

THE END

Other Christian Fiction Books
by Laurie

The Pawleys Island Paradise series:
Book 1: Roadtrip to Redemption
Book 2: Tide to Atonement
Book 3: Journey to Fulfillment
Book 4: Bridge to Fruition
Book 5: Expected in 2016!

Laurie's 2010 EPIC Award Winner for Best Spiritual Romance: Preacher Man

Coming soon! Laurie's 15th anniversary special edition re-release of her very first published novel, *Whispers of the Heart*.

Want to connect with Laurie online? Please do!

Her website/blog
http://authorlaurielarsen.com/

Her Facebook
https://www.facebook.com/authorlaurielarsen

Her Twitter
https://twitter.com/AuthorLaurie

Her Goodreads
https://www.goodreads.com/author/show/412692.Laurie_Larsen

Sign up to be on her newsletter mailing list!
http://authorlaurielarsen.com/newsletter-signup/

About the Author

Laurie Larsen is an empty nester, a 30-year employee of a Fortune 50 company, and the multi-published creator of heartwarming women's fiction. Her 2010 EPIC award-winner, Preacher Man was her first foray into inspirational romance, and now her best-selling series, Pawleys Island Paradise is quickly gaining fans who love heartwarming inspirational love stories. Trips to the beach can now be considered business/research trips – what could be better?